Before
The
Others

102 Moments in Micro Fiction

David Thomas

Also by David Thomas

So Someone Does

ISBN: 978-1-70-705457-2

deaddeerblog.wordpress.com

'But it was you who created that image. Don't you remember? It was you who dreamed up the garden itself. Sometimes I myself feel like a product of your imagination, and I'm afraid that one day you'll make me disappear'

Inês Pedrosa, Nas tuas Mãos.

CONTENTS

DEDICATION

Anna, Claire, Lena, Sevi.

Out of suffering have emerged the strongest souls.
The most massive characters are seared with scars.

MONDAY

A Tale of Two Biddies

It was the best of crimes; it was the worst of crimes. They really didn't think they could pull it off, and indeed they hadn't, perhaps. It was a little early to tell. Certainly the evening had not been carried through without certain elements that were from with-out the plan.

A plan that was startling, if only in its complexity. Honed over several months, conceived and re-conceived over many years, it would be an unlikely situation, one would think, that unforeseen difficulties might arise. It is inevitable, maybe, that a failure to allow ever further expansions, a widening, to consider the Human Factor.

I cannot, and will not, attempt to argue that this plan *did not* allow for the vagaries of the biological machine *at all*, but I will never be convinced that it set out sufficient contingencies for our absurdities.

The blame, you will assume, ought to fall on the head of the canine species, but I find it hard to look in that direction. It is true, as you are all too aware, that the sudden and unexpected apparence of the mutt was the tremor that shifted the beautiful edifice of the plan, rattled its bones, and shimmered its glowering crown until the whole thing was no more than so much sandpaper and nails.

A dog? Did the dog *demand* the attention it received? Maybe. Did a mere floppy-eared, four-legged menace *insist* on the fatal pause for petting?

No, I think not. Biddy is no more. Her plan is no more. And now, I will be now more.

I bid you, adieu.

Pixilated Paintings

Pushing out content, day after day. It was a great idea, once. Take an instantly recognisable classical painting, and render it as if it were produced in the early days of computing. Blocky, but still itself. A good laugh. Friends enjoyed it, and out it went onto social media. It was fun, thinking of new ones, adding amusing quirks to old masters in this heavily pixilated form.

It grew, and some big names started following, eventually even a book was produced. That was fun, but a bit stressful and ultimately of course that type of book is always disappointing. Almost without noticing the pressure to get a new picture out every week (long since stopped doing it daily, how long ago was that?) begin to build. It was no longer fun anymore. The idea was no longer fresh, new ideas for the subversive humour was harder to find. Everyone had seen the gag and moved on.

So a new idea was needed. An equally simple basic concept, and one which could maintain the simplicity of the #pixilatedpaintings identity. Taking some old pixilated graphic games and turning them backwards into old masters was clever, but very difficult, very finite and very niche.

The #pixilatednovels idea was never going to catch on in the modern instant ultra-micro-consumption social media world, and anyway what the hell did it mean?

So. It took months, years even. Cost a fortune and was exceedingly painful but when completed it scored huge in the hits and shares. For a few days. Was it worth it? #pixilatedself trended high for a brief moment, but those uncomfortable square bone alterations were there for life. Never sleep lying down again. #Viral

Gremlins and Girl Scouts

"Hmmmm"

The noise, rather than the words, convinced him that she was in earnest when saying that she would never go back. And if she was never going to go back, then he too would never go back.

Across the street from the Scout Hut lay a formal garden, in the English style. She sat, primly, on a concrete bench as a host of scouts trotted by, in a silence that unsettled her, at once. She was shaking.

He appeared and gradually eased himself onto the bench. She jumped up, startled by his effrontery. Her nerves were shot. Eight months, eight long months, living in that house, had left her in shreds. A shadow of who she once was. He did not understand what had happened there, and he would not ask and she would not tell. But he knew one thing for sure.

They would never go back. Not in this life.

Wafting Waffles

Surprisingly big, are badgers. This particular one (dead it was) more so as it appeared that considerable bloating had taken place. What a sight a badger is! It is an infrequent treat to see one, my own sightings number but three.j Two of these, naturally, were of expired badgers. Big. The first was a wonderfully serendipitous sighting, as we had just turned down the opportunity to enter a wildlife park; the price was, one might say, a trifle above value.

Cycling away, however, we immediately spotted this poor deceased (and diseased) animal. Breath taking. If you don't believe the size, take a look at some trees, the mark where they sharpen their claws. It is high.

So away we rode, flushed with our *free* wildlife (augmented a little later by a *free deer*) and I did not see another one for about fifteen years.

This time I was running in the woods and nearly tripped over it. We were both startled and off it ran, slightly ahead of me. It stuck to the narrow path I run down, convinced I had unkind plans, its little legs spinning as if in a cartoon. It was never in my mind to cause upset or pain, but it could not shake me off, and would not turn away. This spectacle, of a badger at its full speed, pursued by a sweaty middle-aged man continued for slightly longer than it ought to have. Eventually I had to stop. Off it ran, and I did not see another badger for five years.

This one had a splash of blood across its face.

Elevator Love

Arriving home, Mark entered the front room and was startled and concerned by what he saw.

"Claire! What on Earth...... CLAIRE!"

He rushed forward as she crashed to the floor with a sickening bump. Whilst a heavy landing this couldn't, surely, be responsible for all the injuries he could see across his wife's body. Her beautiful eyes were fuzzy, dazed and unfocussed.

"Mark," she half whispered dreamily, concentrating hard, "Claire. Mark and Claire."

"Yes love, that's us. What? What happened? Where does it hurt?"

She smiled, and giggled. "Everywhere."

"Did you trip?" he asked, "You seemed to be in the air when I came in".

"Trip ..." she repeated, looking blankly far away. "Yes, I tripped. Then... then I was ....floating. I was thinking of.... of, oh..... who? Was it Jim? I don't know a Jim. I was just thinking, do I know Jim? Who is Jim? Are you Jim? Who am I? I've forgotten again."

"I'm calling an ambulance." Mark stood up and pulled out his phone, "Well, yes there used to be a Jim out over the other side of the common. I haven't thought of him for *yea* ... Oh yes, ambulance please. Yes, for my wife. My name?"

By now Claire's name had well and truly escaped her and she'd left the floor a little, gently hovering, her crooked limbs gaining some respite as she floated upwards. Mark turned to look at her; something seemed odd. Is she? Yes she is! Dumbstruck he called out to her, long and slow he drew out her name.

Once more, poor Claire crashed to the floor.

Choices or Chances?

Slowly, as the mellow, blurry mist faded, the existential awareness began to sharpen for Jake. The faint, calm, but persistent alarm seeped into his mind, building layers of understanding. The daily renewal had started. Sentient. Human. Bed. Sleep. Day. Jake was back.

The first movements come fitfully, as a bobsleigh team does, back, forth, back, forth, and then off! He swings his legs down and sighs heavily as the feet hit the cold floor. Is the day full of promise, or is it full of obstacles, disappointments? Scratching his head lazily, almost like pushing a button, his mind starts to whirl.

A day full of choices.

Every choice a compromise, every decision shaving something away from his life. Not choices he seeks or desires. His heart sinks as he stands, his eyes avoid the bathroom mirror. At this hour everything is automatic, the coffee appears in his hand magically, his own being not recalling the responsibility it has in its arrival.

Outside, though, the sun is perking up. The coffee is strong and uplifting. Jake sits, with eyes closed again, and his mind empties. A sweet emptiness also erupts around his heart. Maybe, just maybe, this is optimism. This day, these choices, maybe, just maybe, they could be opportunities, he lies to his own clear mind. Jake allows the thoughts back in, one at a time, carefully, building a delicate layered understanding of what he has to do, and how it *could* be alright. Perhaps. He knows, truly knows, it won't be. But he has to survive.

Today, at least.

The Gregarious Gatsby

"Any more, for any more!" echoed across the lawn, high pitched, forced and uneasy. This party was unravelling; it was falling from his hands.

It had not always been like this, of course, not here. His grandmother's tales of the old days would have you believe the grandest of affairs taking place. Late-Victorian mobsters, the Archbishop of Canterbury and at least one disgraced Minister of State all rubbing shoulders, if she were to be trusted.

The old girl, when still *compos mentis*, so this is going back years before her death, would tell one particular story that he would ask for again and again. It concerned a Major Stumble, who claimed to be the first white man to travel the length of the Amazon, a claim that not one single person believed, but all went along with. In fact it was true, but that could not matter less to the society set, for whom image was all, and appearing to be something one was not was rather more satisfying than being somewhat impressive in who you actually were.

The story did not really amount to much, in fact. In essence the Major, rather the worse for wear, deep in the hazy depths of a party and imagining himself back in the Amazon had mistaken a maid for a crocodile.

No one, of course, minded the odd blunderbuss going off, it was a bit of a hoot. The maid was wise enough to go along with it all, and played dead on the banks of the lake. No, the problems arose when she could not resist taking a bite at his ankles.

The Edge of Forever

Introducing ForeverEdge™ the revolutionary new dimension in auto-brinkmanship. Using the latest PlayingWithFire technology™ this all-new system takes the strain out of world-threatening political tomfoolery.

Ideal for the busy demented world leader, simply load in your personal choice of Geopolitcal situation and allow ForeverEdge™ to escalate international relations for you! Kick back and spend more time with your private zoo or commissioning ten metre high statues, safe in the knowledge that someone, somewhere, is stockpiling arms and sabre rattling because of the precision pressure applied by ForeverEdge™.

ForeverEver™ has an intelligent, constantly-updated algorithm that allows you to keep YOUR country at an infinite state of heightened fear and hostility; without ever spilling over into all-out war! *(this feature not guaranteed)*

When you have been enjoying the spoils of power a little too liberally, fear not! ForeverEdge™ overrides any drunken speeches and automatically draws YOUR country back from the brink of commencing world destruction.

Buy ForeverEdge™ today, available at ALL good arms fairs!

ForeverEdge™ – Pushing Leaders' Buttons, So You Don't Have To!

Jellied Geniuses

This should be the last time, he thought to himself as he reached deep into his coat pocket, pulling out the wrinkled paper bag. Striding purposefully, he opened it up, selected a green jelly baby, popped it in his mouth, and returned the bag. His only weakness, he chuckled to himself. Jelly Babies. Always he enjoyed these little treats, except after a 'job'. Then he bought, instead, the large luxury juice-filled fruit jellies that came in lavish boxes of a dozen, at exorbitant prices.

He had her in the boot of the car, and would just need to drive up to the forest to finish it off, and then dump her. As usual he was wholly unconcerned about being observed. That unobtrusive and secluded location where he picked her up, why did so many young hitchhikers like it there?

He tapped on the boot a couple of times as he unlocked the car – shakes them up a bit that does – and switched the radio on, to cover the noise of the banging from the back, which always annoyed him. It is only an hour or so to drive, but then about the same amount of time afterwards, walking. It would not do to leave her too close to the road after all, and besides, he prefers to be undisturbed whilst he, now, how shall we put this? Whilst he 'works'.

He let his mind wander as he drove, it was a beautiful day, in this beautiful countryside, and he thought once again – as he reached automatically for a jelly baby – that she should be his last victim. The thrill was getting less now, it was almost a chore! Thus it was he had only half a mind on the job as he opened the boot to be confronted with the meek, young victim pointing a handgun right at him.

The shock was compounded as he was grabbed from

behind. Soon he was shackled and enduring a long, painful end at the hands of these people. Most of his brain was preoccupied with pain and fear, but he had a little space to wonder where he had seen them before. It was when they started to force-feed him kilos and kilos of jelly babies he recalled their faces.

The owners of the sweetshop knew him well, of course. They kept a good stock of his favourite jelly babies. It took them a few years, but eventually they noticed how they sold an expensive box of fruit jellies every time a young woman went missing – and always to the same individual.

A Ripple in Time

Some things stay in place. It tore in half, even as it tore through the world, and left neither itself, nor anything else, the same ever again.

Of course, as is well established, a small alteration can alter more than a mere … well, a mere what, exactly? And from what perspective is it altered? If it is before, then it is unknown, as it has not yet occurred. From after is more complex.

What has happened now, following the alteration, is, of course, what has, had always happened. So there is no alteration, despite the change. From after it is *also* unknown as it has not *now* occurred.

Throw in a rock. Go on. The present is not so vital, the past not so sacred. History is not set in essential stone, it is just what happened, nothing more. And so what if what happened is now not what had happened, but another happening? It is still history, whichever future point it will have stemmed from, when all is said and done.

Cloudy with a Chance of Grumbles

The Head of the diplomatic service was cautiously optimistic. So far everything had gone very well for the new administration. When the young president had been elected, shortly after the small country had gained independence, there was a lot of concern about security, stability and consensus. Stark charisma is, of course, wonderful at gaining a crushing electoral victory, but only goes so far in building a new country.

At home things had gone quite well, he mused. Rather than unsightly triumphalism the new president had strived for consensus, trying to bring all parties, all people, with him in his vision. The new constitution had been debated and written across the political and, in a stroke of genius, non-political spectrum. This gave it a strength of acceptance, the entire nation having ownership of it, believing in it.

However, it was overseas that President Silme Salaski really scored. In attempting to find a role for his tiny country in the modern global world, he had gone out into it. He had been an instant success, and now his arrival on new shores was eagerly sought and keenly awaited. Approachable, warm, funny and wise he was feted wherever he went. They were on the map, so to speak.

Tonight, though, the ambassador thought, tonight? This is too much. A loss of dignity would be unthinkable for the position of president, and for his country. And thus it was that this country fell to a violent coup. It is possible to say the ambassador operated on good intentions, he just wanted to save his country from ridicule. Now, though, the country is forever remembered as the one that fell apart, as its president was assassinated, moments before appearing on the Morecambe & Wise Christmas Special T.V. show.

The Hitchhikers Guide to Uranus

And so Uranus beget Saturn, and Saturn beget Jupiter, one generation handing on to a larger descendant, each looking further back, out into the darkness, to witness their lesser forbearer.

The inky blackness of space does not allow for true reproduction, these fanciful names handed to solid entities, direct from invented deities. The human capacity for invention and for discovery, a thirst for meaning and a thirst for knowledge married forever, high in the dark sky.

Hitch a ride on a thought. Are we, here on Earth, alone? Is there no one, nothing, out there? There are only two possible answers to this question; both of which are terrifying.

Swimming in Raspberry Jelly

Last night I dreamt of the time I found myself in an hotel room in a situation, and a country, I really should not have been in. Hot and humid, and that was just the cops. The flap of the failing fan fell from the roof and hit my ears, as welcome as a distant newspaper seller. Its lack of cooling power was only matched by that unsoothing noise, flap, flap, flap.

Why they called them "Jelly" here, I'll never know, but "Jellies" they were. Different flavours denoted different ethnicities and a half-forgotten bet from a different life led me to choose differently that night. I called my fixer and he fixed me a Raspberry Jelly.

She knocked lightly at the door, and it swung open. Her open face swung around the room. They'd both seen better days.

Lazily she prowled toward the bed, where I lay, undressed in body and in mind. I motioned her to stop. Her long flowing bathrobe responded to the absence of breeze and remained icily static.

Slowly, coyly, sensuously she untied the cord. I was aroused initially as the robe began its delicious journey off her shoulders, this turned to startled surprise as it hit the floor to reveal the entirety of her body.

It was mine.

The Secret Life of Trees

The lush verdant blanket, from above, has a gently fizzing appearance, and more shades of green than you can possibly dream of. Your dreams are increasingly filled with this forest, initially from a distance, across rich rolling hills, and now in more detail. Each night your restless brain conjures images, ever closer, moving in and above, and finally, moving ever closer with each moonrise.

Slipping into sleep beckons with yet more anticipation, for now your dreams have taken you close onto a single tree. An honest and open tree, its wide branches sitting broadly and comfortably. I am here, this tree says to you, I am here.

The sensation of closing-in never ceases, and tonight you see a leaf as if it were a continent, it fills your mind, and the details magnify and multiple with a heavy inevitability that is welcome, the pressing feel of a woollen blanket on a cold winter's night.

Insects, caterpillars, of course. But these are not the details you crave, these are the giants of the scene, barely comprehensible in their enormity. We see every minute grain of the leaf, the drops of water like oceans, and what life even these contain!

A week further, the nights have shifted and elongated, and the comforting dreamscapes have become unsettling. The varied parts of the atoms may well be awe-inspiring, beautiful even. Yet your rested brain is becoming restless, worried – what lies next?

Sounds of the City

Rich golden rays dribbled noiselessly, perhaps, through the dappled canopy. Birdsong rippled from above. The August sun hung briefly low. The city awakens, yet it be but four o'clock.

Mid-air shimmers, mid-air shimmers, across the park and down through the city. A distant aeroplane hovers. The glint of the sun reflecting on the sharp diamonds, pointing up, pointing up, and pointing out their own importance. Today they rest. It is Sunday.

Disgruntled and dishevelled, Emily pulls away from the sheets and they tumble to the floor. One eye half open a hand flails and encounters half a tab. Still face down she thrusts it in her mouth and lights up. Another day begins. She's gonna start again.

Clinks and mild crashes as she stumbles across the bedroom, the glass detritus of too many nights strewn all around. She slumps onto the toilet. She groans as she pisses. She forgot to bring her fags. She holds her head and sighs. A long and loud sigh, with the disillusionment of one hundred billion dead souls behind it.

In the kitchen she gulps half a tumbler of vodka. The calming rush allows her to reach for the kettle. Cigarette, coffee, clothes. Now Emily is ready to face the sounds of a sleepy city. For Emily, Sunday is her day. Emily has a job to do.

Great Exceptions

Well, I am different aren't I? I must be. I am Great. So if I want to be in this club, I should really lead it, shouldn't I? Well, you all want that really, don't you? You might not realise it, but you are kidding yourselves, I do it better, you don't understand. Well, I agree the rules of the club are all fine, I wouldn't mind adding a few more, ok?

Good, you agree to those ones now? Excellent. Actually they are pretty stupid, now I think about it. Why the hell did you make me follow those rules? Bloody idiots you are. I think it would be better if I don't follow them, myself, just you. Yep? Good then.

And now I think of it, there are lots of rules I don't like in this club. No, I won't pay full subscription fees! Why the hell should *I* pay? Bloody hell. So all agreed, I can pay less? Excellent.

Also those other duties and stuff, some of them I don't want to do. I don't have time. I don't like them. What do you mean I *have* to! I don't have to do *anything* I don't want to. YOU CAN'T MAKE ME. Well, yes, of course, I want to continue to be able to use the clubhouse, get the benefits and all that, obviously, otherwise I wouldn't have let you force me to be a member would I?

OK, so that's all agreed then? I have full access to Club facilities, I have all the benefits and agreements, good. But my subscription fees are less, and some of the rules and duties are not for me. Everyone agreed? Good thank you. Hang on! You arseholes. I'm leaving.

And you *have to* change the rules now, cos they're not fair on a non-club member like me, are they? What?

April Blushes
openly copied and mildly adapted from Amelia Fletcher

Every day she wakes up
Her life will be a movie
All the things she does, written in her diary
But when the day is done, she cannot tell the truth

Pretend her life's exciting
Pretend she'll never lose
April Blush was a present story day
April Blush was a pop celebrity
You can lie to everyone
But please, please don't lie to me

Now she is a popstar
With her own TV show
Tells them all her stories
And hopes they'll never know

Now her life's exciting
Now she'll never lose
Don't be anybody else
Forget about the rest
You'll always be April
You'll always be yourself

April runs every day
Her life runs by too fast
All the things she hides, written in the papers
April blushes to read them, she cannot tell the truth

April Blush is a present story day
April Blush is a pop celebrity
She lied to everyone
But why, why did you lie to me?

Now April lies for all time
Her life was like a movie
All the things she did, written in a billion words
And now her star has sunk, who can tell the truth?

Was her life exciting?
Did she win or lose?

*I enjoyed doing this one a lot, a real lot. But it must be noted straight
away that most of the words, and most of the ideas are not my own.
Influence? Adaptation? Theft? You decide.*

TUESDAY

Flowering Fields of Fortune

Even before the first shoots emerged, he himself was underground, a body used up and worn out before its time.

A fruitless life tilling the soil. Hard, hard work, and always an eye out for the chance, the shortcut to riches that would allow him to rest, even one day, even one lie-in. Farming was all he had known, however, and every pound he sowed into a new plan was lost three times over.

So back to the land. The daily grind. The seasons turned and the melancholy routines never changed. And every harvest yielded yet less return. Why the price of everything continually rose, with the one notable exception of his own crops, was a question that ate away at him morning, noon and night, seven days a week, winter, spring, summer and autumn.

Property, specialist breeds, farm-experience holidays, music festivals, pyramid schemes, he had tried it all. His spectacular failings were down to a particularly piquant combination of his ill luck, his ill timing, and his commitment to being ill-informed.

He ploughed thousands into property, weeks before the crash. He joined a huge and profitable 'airplane game' at the seventh level and was milked at an efficiency he could only dream of for his cows.

A lifetime of the dashed hopes, failures and hard work left his brain partially cracked and when a plausible rogue offered him 10,000 'magic' pennies for only 5,000 pounds he couldn't resist. The long-haired, long-bearded con-man donned his druidical robes to incant over the pennies, genuine ones, as it happens, he had collected that morning from the bank. Our hapless hero thanked him and ploughed them into his land, there and then.

Sadly that very night he expired. Eight months later excited neighbours carefully guarded the secret they stumbled upon on the land of the irascible old farmer, who had died without issue, wholly alone.

They soon found the buds resembled pennies, and if left would blossom into larger coins, and eventually grow into notes. As they grew and matured the transformation continued, eventually the fruits fluttering to the floor creating a carpet of beautiful, legal, fifty pound notes.

And Larry, the con artist? Dear reader, you will be, I trust, pleased to hear he never discovered the delicious con that nature had played upon *him*, just as he was conning our desperate farmer.

Nicked Nails

The boxes stacked long and high were a fascinating section of the huge ironmongery outlet, each one stuffed with different sized (and tipped) nails. First, and bewilderingly, it was assumed you would have a knowledge of what type you wanted, and how they differed. This was beyond me; I just wanted some so long, more or less, and for wood, but also to go in the wall. I was putting up shelves.

Having found your nails, the next task was to get a handful, stick them in a bag, and weigh them. Again I was unsure exactly how many I would need. Three shelves, four to a shelf, maybe, plus a couple for the inevitable bent ones caused by poor hammer work. Fourteen seemed an oddly specific and small number, so I stuffed another bunch in, knowing fine well that they would sit for all eternity in the back of my drawer, *that* drawer.

Even with the additional ones, the paper bag felt insecure and insignificant, so I slipped it into my pocket, rather than the basket. I had weighed them and delighted in their cheapness.

On arriving home I plunged my hand into my coat pocket and discovered I had forgotten to put them through to be scanned. The shelves and tools preoccupied me and they slipped my mind. Never mind their value was low; I had entered the world of the criminal.

****

I can never really know, of course, not *really*. I am a tremendously poor craftsman, and the shelves were wonky and unstable when I finished. At least they were up, I reasoned, and my books sat happily on them. It was strange

27

though, it *was* weird.

It was around a week later that the first one worked its way out and dropped to the floor. I heard the tinkle. The next couple I did not notice, not until later anyway. I know I am bad at this, but I cannot see how they could possible work their way out, but this they did. Every single one of the nicked nails threw itself out of the wall, one by one, as if my guilty conscious resided within them, and sent my shelves and beautiful books crashing to the floor.

The Blue Screen of Death

The water lay heavy on her skin. When she had plunged her porcelaine-white hand in, the warmth enveloped it, and the slightest hint of colour drew over her fingers. That was some hours previously, and Kanchini had sunk into a thought cycle every bit as deep as the heated natural pool.

Where she was, physically, was stunningly beautiful yet where she was internally was not. Her mind dragged her back, and it dragged her around and around, even as she lay, inert, not even the hint of a ripple emanated from her position. With eyes closed, all is black: and so she closed her eyes. The rich deep blue of the pool, the stunning and varied verdant forest all around, these were not the hues for her mood.

The actions taken against her (whether they were directed at her or not is immaterial) were cruel and relentless. She had had enough. She processed each and every slight, each and every mark, she was bruised and battered across her body, and throughout her soul and in her mind. Her head aches, she could sense the damaged thoughts smashing around her skull and it *hurt*.

Kanchini was done. Her eyes closed, her resolve finally smashed. As she sank down, her head broke the blue screen of water and entered the warm embrace. Never to return. A tortured soul searching peace. Yet no peace, no, not even there.

Bristly, yet Sensible

The screech of a magpie startled her, and she sensibly, instantly, en-rolled. Curled up in her own warmth and darkness, her inadequate eyes darted to and fro, her breathing sharp and uneven. How long before the danger passed? Listening intently, the flap of the wing told her that the threat had taken flight. Gently she unrolled.

Once more encompassed within her thoughts of food, she snuffled under the bushy, green, rich, hedge. The black point of her coned face twitched; a worm met its end, wriggling and squirming through the hot pinkness of her mouth, and down through blackness, toward its final destiny.

Next some fungi, fruit and a treat of a juicy snail. This was a feast indeed. Snorting happily, she foraged and ate as the night waned towards dawn. It was time to sleep. Within a short eighteen hours, she would be up again, bristling with her quiet, unassuming, solitary ways.

Animalia
Bilateria
Deuterostomia
Chordata
Vertebrata
Gnathostomata
Tetrapoda
Mammalia
Theria
Eutheria
Erinaceomorpha
Erinaceidae
Erinaceinae
Erinaceus europaeus

A Moose on the Loose

A great cry of intense distress sang across the wide plains, as the searing pain of an exploded tooth screams across your brain. Something was afoot. From this vast distance it was a mere speck, but one that appeared to be moving with purpose. Striding out in torn and tattered clothes, she headed directly toward the sound.

This was the enigmatic 'S'. Her face covered, more or less, she appeared, she solved, she moved on. No one knew who, how or why. On this occasion there was none to witness her doings, none bar you and I, dear reader. Together we will try and construct the events from what we find, a story of sorts, a version that holds water.

Water. There is very little of that out here. What do we find? No footsteps, no sign, except the silver-white bones half-buried. From the skull we may assume a moose, but how? What on earth would a moose be doing *here*.

To recap: 'S' has been; a scream has been heard; a moose's flesh has been picked away.

She does not come for no reason. She does not leave until a job is done. She speaks not, she never deigns to explain. She does. She sorts. She saves.

But what? Here? What here?

Where the Wild Things Aren't

The creak of ancient trees shuddered softly across the countless squat crosses. The low, dark rows, marking six thousand final resting places. Blossom fluttered by, a gentle gust of wind shaking it loose.

Far away, across the fields and highways, the underpass has a not atypical aroma. Half-light, piss, fear and resignation all combine in this useful cave. Useful, yes, yet ridden with dejection. A close atmosphere somehow keeps the air at bay, despite the yawning entrances.

Even here, a beach, a beautiful, rich yellow beach, the sun beginning its decline, after a day's work of warming the world. A new job begins, as it dazzles those reclining with its own setting. Myriad colours, changing, moving, even as they progress ever darker. Yet even here, yes even here, there is little joy. Satisfaction, perhaps, a bittersweet sadness for yet another perfect day gone, lost.

The heavy machinery starts its insistent drone. The first ground is broken. all flora and fauna banished. Gleaming, new, concrete. Man is here. Wild things are not.

The Boy without a Name

Sitting on the steps he watched the wall in front of him. A tiny crack in the plaster, perhaps, had appeared in the last weeks, low down along the bottom, toward the right. Closely studying this day after day, week after week, every single nuance in the paint was familiar.

As his age progresses, his world does not. These stairs, this wall. The seasons come, move, pass, yet they are unknown to our young friend. He switches himself off, he becomes nothing. This is how the time passes. He is dimly aware as figures pass him, up, down, these blurred figures have things to do, places to be. He cannot allow himself to think of this or his own inaction, solitude becomes more acute.

And then, one day, one speaks to him. He stares, bewildered. A yellow bucket dangles in front of him. The unfamiliar sound of a voice barely penetrates. Slowly, carelessly, his muscles tense as he attempts an unused memory; to stand.

Yet his body cannot cope with this foolish, futile attempt to rise. He sighs and stumbles. His hands flail and he cannot steady himself, down and down he goes, flight after flight.

Rocket Launching Ladies

It took far too much time, but at least now the immense contribution made by remarkable female mathematicians to the NASA Apollo missions is very well known.

What is less well known, however, is that it was a woman who first came up with the idea of faking moon landings, and was the *de facto* mission controller that oversaw a success so great that many people still believe it was genuine, even to this day.

By the late 50s it was obvious to all that the Soviet Union was way ahead in the so-called 'Space Race', and Kennedy's special advisor Marge Winkledoon felt this was a weakness he could utilise to win the election, and having done so she further felt it essential to deliver on it. It was she who wrote the iconic 'We choose to go to the Moon' speech (JFK himself adding the Rice/Texas football gag), and when it became increasingly obvious that the States had no hope of achieving this goal, she was tasked with heading up an ultra-secret committee to explore solutions.

The USA had nether the technology, nor the know-how to take a human to the Moon (and back) before the end of that decade; it simply did not exist. Even the Soviets could not have done so. One day, date unknown, Winkledoon delivered her fresh approach to a stunned committee. It was going to be very tough, it was going to need as few people in the know as possible (even most individuals on the project did not know the reality), but she was convinced she could pull it off. And boy, did she!

Those people present, had they been able to see into the future half a century later, would never have believed her gamble could have paid off. They thought she was nuts when she uttered the immortal line that started the drive to the sham Apollo 11 mission. To a deadly silent room, deep under the New Mexican desert, she calmly stated her case.

"We'll fake it."

Lord of the Pies

Gazing at the stars, the pie-crust breeched, the king of pies is set in place, the centre-piece of both the meal and the table. Cheery twittering, and a few giggles as it arrives, the beady dead eyes, marking a ring of tiny black spots, almost an eerie, dark halo encircling the browned, crisp crust.

Yet the obvious pathos of the morbid scene is lost on those who gasp with delight. For these diners, in clothes that are fine, yet not fancy, this is nothing but a joy. Their own beady eyes, very much alive, and lively, roam again and again across the absurd spectacle.

Lips are even licked, the host sighs a satisfied sigh and calls loudly that it is time for him, himself, to serve up. What bizarre ritual is this, the cheery demeanour as the languid, lifeless form of the once glorious, swimming, silver flash, icily beautiful in the cool water, is laid gently, grotesquely in front of each ample stomach. How different, this drab plate in this pallid room.

Consumed, lukewarm.

The Bridge to Malawi

It is not, in fact, a bridge, it is the sun. But the exquisite symbolism is irresistible. So let us call it a bridge. How many other countries can boast a bridge on their flag? None. None at all, in fact, as this one is, as we have seen, actually the rising sun, a sun rising on the hopes of African nations gaining independence.

The blood-red and Mother Nature green set to the uncompromising black, now at the top of the flag. Rising suns and arching bridges, rich in meaning. But what actual bridge could span the mighty Lake Malawi?

Well, let us now consider the famous bridge in the north of the country, crossing the Rukuru. It is, somewhat prosaically, described as a pedestrian bridge. It is, let us be honest, alarming. With its bamboo and vine construction, rickety and unstable, yet still standing after all these years, it truly is a wonderful metaphor for those states across the great continent and their independence. And also their precious and undervalued individuality. Long may it stand, and long may this warm heart beat.

Blue Jean's Babies

She wasn't a Tory. She had a fairly run-of-the-mill shade of skin. She wasn't a Toffee, or a Citizen, she didn't even have blue eyes. But for some reason, lost in the midst of time, Jean was always known as 'Blue' Jean.

It was owing to the nickname, rather than the other way around, that she painted her house a vibrant blue. Jean had a heart the size of Mount Everest and an ocean of kindness to give. Jean brought joy and a pleasant word to everyone's day. She enriched every life she touched. And this became a vast number of lives. Out of great disappointment Jean could wring great happiness.

Her own inability to have children was a sadness she buried deep deep inside but one that never truly left her. She took this pain and used it to fearlessly and determinedly take on every young life she could. Whether abandoned or orphaned, whether the mother was too young, or scared, or bewildered to cope, Jean would step in. That beautiful big house was full for decades with the sounds of young lives, starting out. Crying, laughing, playing. She had time for them all and she never forgot one; and not a single one of Blue Jean's Babies forgot Jean, or her blue house, for their entire lives.

The Last Link

Links in a chain. One moves to the next, each an individual with all their hopes and fears, and yet the chain is nothing unless each and every one is strong, maintained, sturdy.

I am the flaky link in this whole chain, the point at which it is most likely to break. Yet I feel I have the most pressure exerted on me, under the most strain. Perhaps not, from another angle maybe I am, in fact, the link who is *exerting* the pressure. I am not so sure.

Round and round and round it rolls. I see no way forward, none back, but still it rolls round and around. No end. An end, with no end.

She walks, disconsolately, in the drizzle, wondering what and where and how and who and when and why. No, not why. She knows why.

A dog charges out, it is on its lead, but no one is at the other end. She whips around, chases, plunges her foot forward, slamming it onto the end of the lead, the last link. The dog jerks in full flight, suddenly seized by great force around the *neck*. A horrific surprise, in the midst of such joy. It yelps. The chain breaks. For a moment they stare, at each other. Time stands still. Who will recover first?

They move.

Uneasy Aubergine Episodes

In fact, the ground *did* open up and swallow me.

It was all a misunderstanding, see? I did not mean it like that and of course I was mortified. I would like to say 'I don't know who was more embarrassed', but I do. It was me. *He* seemed to enjoy it, which was, of course, worse. What an awful situation to be in, with him being my boss, effectively, and all.

I do not even know how I came to be running such an absurd errand in the first place. I'm actually on the creative side, but there was this big launch, see? Lots of the Big Nobs from the States were over, and of course he was desperate that it went well. Nothing he loved more than rubbing shoulders with the high and mighty from his homeland.

Oh yes, he's a yank alright. That is where trouble began. I was pretty angry that he asked *me* to run to the *shops* to get some stuff to serve, but then, it was 'all hands on decks', as it were, and he himself was sweeping and mopping the board-room, so I could not really complain, could I?

Why the fuck is it an 'eggplant' anyway? It makes no bloody sense. I did not bother checking the list until I was there, everything else was quite straightforward. I was not quite sure about that. I had no idea what on Earth how he planned to prepare or serve it at such short notice, so I thought maybe I had misunderstood. I sent a text to check.

To avoid any further problems I simply sent an icon, an emoji, with a question mark. A long pause before a reply, and it was a reply that frankly startled me.

I had no idea. Once I discovered what it all meant I nearly died, and longed for the ground to open up and swallow me.

Which it did. He still texts, lurid and awful texts. But I'm not coming out. Not ever.

A New Fallen Snow

The morning breaks, crisp, pure, and bright. A new dawn, a restart, a rebirth. All is muffled, the bright gleam is both compelling and challenging to the sight, yet seems to dull the other senses. One it sharpens, the others it leaves confused and woolly.

Everything needs to be clear, in a row. However keenly occupied the eyes are, what needs to be seen is hidden from view. Trying to unpick the truth, without sight or sound, with no taste, merely a cold sensation and only an unintelligible white smell; it is so hard, so very, very hard.

Think now. Think. Thoughts. Take control of those thoughts. This landscape must be understood, laid clear, *in a row*. It is an intellectual process, perhaps, and can be understood, without recourse to the senses, surely?

But this clogging snow is no more than the harsh, brittle, frozen incompetence of thought. Untamed, inaccurate, inexhaustible and failing notions filling the brain, creating those huge, dark, storm clouds, that lead inexorably to the fall of suffocating snow, deep, crisp, and even now, holding you back.

A Simple Reason Was All She Needed

An unfeasibly long drawn out explanation was forthcoming (my uncle is worse) yet all that was really required was something that could be thrown off in a couple of lines.

It had all started, of course, with her absurd attempts at ghostly behaviour. "The bones are unsettled", she would wail, a promising start. Not long after however she was testily stating, in quite a normal voice, that "all horrors would be seen before long in front of the Super-Saver", a most un-ghostly vision. She had even got hold of some chains to rattle, but being of the white plastic variety dread was not instilled.

So why, I hear you ask, these attempts at spooking us? The explanation was simply that she was bored, the only excuse she needed for anything (remember the incident with bedsheets, broken hinges and almonds in Consdorf? Who could forget).

Yet she would cut out her tongue before admit that. Hence her hour-long description of an increasingly unlikely series of coincidences that she claimed, quite erroneously, led to her stumbling around the High Street at half past five on a Tuesday afternoon declaring, "The fetid remains of long forgotten Guinea Pigs will return at midnight". Luckily no one was around to see her and soon she settled down to sleep, at home, in a box marked "Maxwell House, Premium Blend 24 x 250g – NOT FOR RESALE". By morning she had done with ghosts, and went for a fairly uneventful five kilometre jog.

Funnily enough, some rotten undead Guinea Pigs *did* return to that village, but not until a couple of weeks later.

Trendy Traditions

Authentic and original. Both meanings of those words being heavily corrupted. Yet another trendy place with a new-fangled, old-fashioned twist. We are here again. I wonder if there is any mileage in nostalgia for the previous nostalgic crazes? The Young-Fogies, The Beatles as Edwardians, should we hark back to the 'original' or the harkers-back themselves?

And what's so wrong with long beards and, heavy iron roasting machines? Well, nothing of course. What is worse, perhaps, is demanding authenticity in inauthentic traditions. We gaze with wonder, or incredulity, at any British Royal event, be it coronation, wedding, birth or funeral, and yet those who love or loathe rarely know how modern these 'timeless' and 'immortal' traditions are, most of them, dreamt up by Prince Albert.

Last night I dreamt that Cliff Richard had grown a very long, very straight, grey moustache. A blessed relief, in fact, from my now traditional dream, which untraditionally reflects all too accurately life itself. How very uncool.

Her Name Was Elle

I saw her, she fell.
An elegant ankle, turned
Black skirt, black tights, black shoes.
Standing there, I too fell.
Her name was Elle.

I rushed, where she fell,
She whimpered, I asked,
You hurt? You need? You want?
Helping there, I too fell.
Her name was Elle.

WEDNESDAY

Anne of Gruesome Gables

The body was found in the grounds, away from the house, over amongst the broad, ancient oak trees. A startled cry heralded the discovery, on that chilly, wet, April evening. (The authorities were called, arrived and busied themselves, making a lot of noise, it seemed to old Mrs. Hardacre, and a lot of mess). She ruefully considered an old adage, as she hunched in the rain, watching the activity, as so many uniforms rattled around the copse, concentrating on their own small tasks and not a single one gaining any notion at all of what had happened.

Death, it was, that had happened. A young life completed, far too early, perhaps. Despite the time passing, despite the tape, the tent, the photographs, the notes (the endless notes), still no-one had any idea whose soul had owned and used that body. *Almost* no-one, thought Mrs. Hardacre, as she heard yet another car approach along the shingle drive, a gently rolling crunch building in a familiar, gentle way, culminating with a louder, final, sound as the vehicle came to an uncertain stop.

But this car was different. No sirens, no markings, small, grey, indistinct. Out stepped a woman, a woman of medium height, with hair that was neither long, nor short, and a beige mac that had surely (one would hope) seen better days.

Mrs. Hardacre gave her little thought, journalist maybe, or just a ghoulish passer-by. Mrs. Hardacre should maybe have paid more mind to the driver of the grey two-door, for this was her nemesis. How could Mrs. Hardacre have known this was the principal authority, the sharpest (if troubled) mind for many miles around. This was Anne. And she was here to solve.

Outlandish Suggestions

"You wouldn't dare!"

"She'll be furious, us being late again, we must say something". The elder child was the boldest. Little did she know her entire life would be shaped by today.

"I'm scared," the youngest had the strongest faith, "it is wrong to talk like this."

"Well it's this, or another beating off mother."

And so it was, upon arriving home and receiving the anticipated wrath of their parent, their carefully prepared statement was delivered. To their initial relief, and eventual horror, they were believed. Not only at home, but in the village, throughout the country and in time around the world. Yes, even in the Vatican.

From then on, the huge engine of religious industry took over and before long the revenue generated demanded that the children were trusted. Two of the children were so uncomfortable with it all, they were about to reveal all, and tell the truth. She silenced them, for good, and enjoyed the long and happy life of a religious superstar.

Today I wrote in Fatima, Portugal. Any resemblance to other stories in these parts is purely coincidental and this is in no way intended to be an outlandish suggestion as to what happened a hundred years ago. At all.

Slipping between the seams, there was no turning back

Seemingly too late she rushed at the building and managed to push through the throng to the front. Shouting over the voices, waving her hands in front, she secured a ticket somehow and ran out the back. The doors of the bus were closing, but she banged on them and the driver, in no hurry himself, opened them.

It appeared considerably more probable that the people squeezed inside would burst out the door than her entering, but somehow she did. "There's always room for one more", the driver chuckled. It occurred to her that this could not possibly be true, but at least she was on board, and they were off. It was extraordinarily uncomfortable.

It ought to have been a blessed relief to get moving, the still air thick with heat and sweat. However, as the bus picked up speed the open windows served only to swirl the thick sweaty air around.

Well, this was it. The ticket had cost her the majority of what she had left. No chance of a return ticket. Bridges burnt. Like so many before her she found the city beckoning. What awaited her she knew not.

Waving her granddaughter off several decades later she thought back to that day. Full of promise it was, but she could harldy believe that it was she that had taken such a plunge. It worked out, of course, eventually. The first years were hard, horrific even. No, don't think about that time. Think about what came later.

There was no turning back then, and there was no turning back now, from the fresh horrors awaiting her in her beautiful old home. She was so worried for her granddaughter as she set off, the thought that she should be worried for herself could not have been further from her mind.

Still; Go, know.

Phosphorescent Filaments

The rags had been soaked and stuffed, he just needed to drag the tiny stick across the sand and glass, causing an instant reaction, toss it in, turn and get out of there. This he did. He breathed in. A short pause before the noise and heat erupted in front of him. He span around and ran.

The flames rose and flickered, strong, agile, fearsome. They took hold and grew, both in size and resilience. Yet still the building resisted. The façade was gone, but like the very kebabs it once served, the central structure remained intact as the outer layers were untidily eaten away.

Amid the black smoke the heat was white. The creak of the hot metal as it groaned and twisted reflected the owner, far away and unaware, restlessly fighting for death in the hospice, his distressed family all around. Many hours later they left the scene of one destructive tragedy, only to arrive at another.

The Kissing Curse

It was not the rain, perhaps, that led to the problems. If we are content to call them 'problems'. I cannot lie; I did tremendously well, financially, from what happened, although of course I did have to deny it, back then. It is unlikely that anyone believed my version, but of course it was unnecessary that they should. It was enough that it had been said.

I suppose he was not the first to be undone by a kiss. A simple peck on the cheek, that was that. We must allow that this was a simple, natural, act; A greeting of friendship. How could they have known where it would lead? Maybe if they had stayed outside, this would not have occurred. But again, can we blame nature? It was only a light and brief drizzle, after all.

The response was as swift as it was understated. I do not need to underline how unfortunate we all felt it was (or, as I say, how fortunate, in other ways) but it is a point that we must not labour. I cannot stand mawkishness, it looks bad and makes me queasy.

And so it was that one more soul was sent on its way, betrayed by a kiss. As ancient as the world, is the need for companionship, as deadly as the scorpion can this be. It looks like it is getting out nice this afternoon, I may take a solitary stroll.

Hold Your Hankering Horses

The desire was too much to contain. Zoom in as everything else around that troublesome target loses focus, becomes fuzzy, indistinct and eventually disappears. Ceases to be. Hence it is that all around is torn down, laid to waste, gone to waste. Decaying or destroyed, it is all the same. A full-on desperate charge toward this fatal, foolish whim.

Inside, though, it is uncontrollable, unstoppable. Nothing, but nothing, matters. Everything and everyone can go to hell, and do.

$$* \qquad * \qquad * \qquad *$$

Turning the corner, a corner like any other, out on the country path and suddenly face to face with it. Let us get one thing straight from the off; horses are *big*. This one had steam in its nostrils and blood in its mane. And it was angry. The shimmering, rock hard muscles rippled and strained as it reared and snarled.

$$* \qquad * \qquad * \qquad *$$

"What did you do to contribute? To help?"

Can you respond? What *did* you do? Drink and complain? Rant and read? Did it help? Did any of it help? The distant sun revolves softly and gently sinks. You are left in the dark of the dusk and the silence of your soul. You failed. You know you have failed and all that is left is to stare at that realisation of who and what you are, amongst the bleak ruins of a longing that is long-lost. You did not make it, you see now, you did not hold back yet neither did you succeed.

A waste. An all-encompassing waste. Too much, too late.

Criss-Cross Applesauce

Any Luxembourger worth their salt would certainly be cross if you served them up some *gromperekichelcher* without any apple sauce. The cool, sharp, stodgy compote contrasts, and compliments, the crispy, *very* hot, and wonderfully delicious potato cakes perfectly.

And all Luxembourgers are in reflective and mournful mood, as one of their number has passed away, and with him a tangible link to history, and to *the* event in this small country's modern identity.

The Grand Duke Jean has died, having some years ago abdicated in favour of his son, as his mother, the revered and venerated Grand Duchess Charlotte, had previously for him. During the second war the Royal Family were in exile, led by Charlotte raging a highly successful diplomatic, propaganda and morale-boosting war of her own throughout the free world.

Finally the allies were ready to liberate Luxembourg, urged on by US President FDR who had made a personal assurance to Charlotte, who had become great friends to the American First Family. Her husband, Felix, and Jean had joined the British Army whilst in exile and were amongst the troops entering the Grand Duchy. Wild scenes ensued. Not only were Allied Forces securing Luxembourg, but members of the Royal Family itself were there, on Luxembourgish soil. Liberation was assured, and the people knew that they could, in the famous and memorable motto, 'remain what we are'.

This picture shows the-then Prince Jean (centre, in uniform, with beret) being mobbed as the troops entered the city, to liberate the country from German occupation, September 1944

Jean, Grand Duke of Luxembourg

5th January 1921 – 23rd April 2019

Hippopotamus Expectations

Working forwards tended to result in more satisfying outcomes but it was not always possible. Aim low, and the chances of disappointment will also be lower. This may, or may not be true, but what we do know is that Juan had only modest expectations.

From the outset this project was a half-arsed, half-formed, after-thought. Juan himself certainly would not even call it, or consider it, anything so grand as a 'project'. It was just a thought, a semi-idea that came to him one Tuesday afternoon, but it was enough for him to turn it over and spend an hour or so trying to see if it might work. He was unsurprised, and barely disappointed, to discover it would be doomed.

'Surely you have to succeed, if you give everything you have.'
Penelope Fitzgerald, The Bookshop

An achingly sad line, and Juan is busy proving the exact opposite right here. Failure in one field, however, does not mean failure in all. Barely thinking about what he had started, and certainly with no follow-up initially, it was some time before he even noticed what was happening.

When he looked, he found it had grown. This encouraged him to give it an hour or two smoothing out some obvious problems. It continued to grow and grow outside of his control. Juan had given almost nothing and become a sensational success.

What lessons for life do Juan, his creation, and his story give us? Try everything you think of? Don't give it your all? Throw enough pebbles and you'll hit a duck, one day? Fortune favours the lazy?

Silver Sand

Many years of solid service is what had secured his reputation, his status within a community. There was, I suppose, an element of irony about his downfall.

Irony, not meaning something having the quality of iron, was a good example of why he never bothered. Even during the long years, mourning his son, he never bothered.

I must state also that downfall is a word that is too strong here. Mr. Breven carried on with his work as the only pharmacist in the town and continued to enjoy the custom of many people in that town. Not everyone, of course, but many. Enough for him to see out his active years behind the counter, and even eek out a modest retirement. A retirement of reflection, during which he still did not concern himself to learn.

A medical man (of sorts) who cannot read, nor write, is not quite the problem you may imagine. Certainly on arriving in this town I suspected nothing and then, some years later, arriving upon the knowledge of Mr. Breven's lack of knowledge I was surprised. Dismayed maybe. I even offered, obliquely, to teach him. He misunderstood my overture however, and thought I had invited him to lunch.

Thus it was that he and I enjoyed lunch every third Thursday, at my expense, for some thirty years until his timely death. Enjoyable lunches, all, at which we discussed every subject under the sun, whether philosophy and art, or sport and politics. Or, rather I should say, these conversations covered *almost* every possible topic, all in fact, save one.

We never once spoke of the fateful day on which his illiteracy led to him selecting 'Silver Sand' in error, whilst making up a delicate prescription.

This substance is, of course, a fatal poison to all, not least to Mr. Breven's only son, the late Ernest Breven.

The Sanctuary of Subtleties

Flailing around, sharply jerking from one side to the next like a headless Pegasus, The Cork-Hawk was clearly not as it ought. Coming into port, with a over-full cargo of pork had never been so fraught. Up on the poop deck Captain Debt loomed out of the bright room, and into the gloom. The boat *had* to make safe anchor, if the skilled banker could keep it afloat.

Captain Seb, with his fork, had fled, toward Sark. He stalled, he had to call, he had to shout before the fall, he came about, the waves receded, it was the chance he needed.

On the dock, amongst the cod, was a slight light, never yet awed, odd. In that pure sanctuary was a sight to see, to lure, through the fog. Indeed, in flight, attempted but fought (in deed, dour), the Cap'n could not see, for it was, YES, it was she – the headless Pegasus.

Not All Tarts Are Raspberry

When all the tarts, all the pies, all the cakes were brought out a gasp went around the room. It was an intriguing idea, even if it risked the ire of many a guest. The pies were all open top, the cakes heavily iced. But every single one was red in colour. Cherry pies, strawberry cakes, raspberry tarts. Not all the tarts were raspberry, of course. Every red fruit imaginable was represented. Cranberries, pomegranates, even red grapes and red apples.

It was an incredibly striking effect. The shades of red glowing and glistening in the bright lights, a hundred diners gasping and laughing. Well, ninety-nine. The sight of all these beautiful desserts did nothing for one old duffer, parked away in the corner, but still with his deep, booming, foghorn voice.

"What the devil?" he barked, "I like apricots."

The Cuckoo's Falling

A siren. A gentle, distant, whoosh as something falls rapidly from high. The thud that follows. Sounds screaming and bellowing and pulsating through the night. A city that never sleeps, a million stories that are yet but one.

Everyone in the city is on the move, no one stays still for long, and all of them headed in the exact same direction. The ultimate goal, not always desired, an own-goal in fact whether sought or not, the final terminus, as each of the city's key moving parts ricochet apart, and the bits that were us are spread out into an eternal void.

The endeavour of life, it may be concluded, can be summarised in a few parameters: reproduction; growth; respiration and so on. This can be pared down, however, to one overarching and unavoidable truth. If something can die, then it has life. And everything that can die, will die.

And as I watch this cuckoo falling for a fleeting moment I am struck, the bird swoops today. And I swoop with it. I am no more.

Funky Fetishes

Collecting the key was more complicated than expected. A semi-hidden and deeply troubling bar, down a mean alley off side-street, which was rather difficult to find. It was also a little disturbing, given the object of the task, like sitting in a hot queue of cars to reach a beauty spot. It just felt wrong.

But once the grimy barman had handed over the key, gurning hideously and suggestively, she decided to press on. She'd come this far, she reasoned, and it had seemed such an unusual, exciting, turn to take. It was not like her at all, not *at all*. Lisa was looking for something to take her out of herself, 'shake her bones' after such a crushing series of disappointments, something had to change. Why not try this?

So now Lisa found herself down yet more unfamiliar streets, was she lost or did she *want* to be lost? Eventually, inexorably the address arrived in front of her. Deep breathe. Fumble the key. Wishing so hard that it doesn't fit, it doesn't turn.

But turn it does, and almost despite herself she enters. She wants to try this, to be someone else for a while, someone so very different, she is determined to try it.

Now she is in the tiny room, however, she is not so sure. But she had promised herself to try it. Just this once. No one would know. Hold your breath, Lisa old girl, give it a whirl, it was like a mantra in her head, a head she was trying so hard to keep clear, vivid, sharp. Here goes.

She gulped deeply, and she knelt.

A Gambler and a Thief

"In order to gain something you have to lose something. Stealing things from others in order to live is even more painful."
Genki Kawamura, If Cats Disappeared from the World

"I just want to be happy."

Is there any more pathetic intention than that? Happy? Those who have no idea what unhappiness, genuine unhappiness is, squeaking about being 'happy'.

Not having food in your belly, not being able to put food in your children's bellies. That's unhappiness. A vague sense of middle-aged discontent after a comfortable and secure fifty or sixty years with twenty, thirty, forty more ahead. Unhappy? Don't make me laugh.

But they can convince themselves it is enough, it is real. And by the time they take action, they have further convinced themselves it is not even a gamble. No risk. It happens to anyone. No one will judge me, and if they do, how bloody dare they? Before long they see themselves, not a gambler and a thief, but as Noble Heros caught up in an unfair world in which they battle courageously to the take the moral high ground.

What horrific perversion of reality is this? Their made-up notion of their happiness, and the import of their own happiness above all else, is not, of course, a personal thing. To gain it they must lie, cheat and above all thieve. Take what is not theirs.

How can they live with themselves? How can they live? Painful to live whilst taking from others? Indeed, but not painful for them - For they are 'happy'.

Purposeful Pinches

"It's not like he has any dogs in this game, is it? I mean, why busting my neck on this?"

Joel carefully selected the third cigarette in the pack, slid it out and leisurely lit it. He drew deeply on it, paused and thought before he spoke precisely.

"Ah, forget about it, you know him. He's all about the details and *all* about the shit. He loves giving people shit. It's your turn. You're it, you're the it-shit."

The bleak, sporadic lighting of a closed parking lot barely warmed the whiteness of their weathered faces. Josh leaned on the wheel.

"Fuck it, anyways, what's he want us to do, though? Always with the what's happening, what's happening? but he don't tell me nothing."

"Sit tight. Always the answer, Josh old buddy. If in doubt, sit tight."

So they sat, and they grumbled and they smoked and they watched. Night after night after night. "Nothing is happening," complained Old Ted to them, from behind his thick curtain of cigar smoke, "and it's happening too fast."

Just like that it happened. Just another night. And it happened, in the end, slowly, drawn out. The job was on, it was live. Josh perhaps had time to register it, Joel probably not, as they became the first (of 28) victims of the Smart Grass Heist, long before it had even garnered that inaccurate moniker.

Peach Coffee and Hazelnut Tea

The milk has mint, the "speciali-tea" has the mint-milk *and* rosemary and for the kids? Sage-ade. The beards desperately long to be timeless but are oh-so achingly of their time.

Moka-almond-espresso-creamy-cookie-float, with added biscuits fingers and doritos. If some is good then more *must* be better, right? Coffee is water-weak and comes in buckets. A horrendous mix of many cultures and none. Who in their right minds wants breakfast cereal in an iced coffee? Yet they come. And the prices! A single bath of insipid coffee can set you back more than a meal.

Pity the poor sap, in desperate need of non-inebriating cheer after a long day, who pops into the bewilderingly decorated and overly-knowing café, then shuffles to the counter with the words, "A nice cup of tea, please."

Some fucking luck.

Illuminating Illustrations

Illuminating rides through the shadows,
Flicking in and out of the sharp light
The unsettling dark, brought to fore
meadowfuls of fundamental insight.

Cranial cavity holds more than is able,
pulsing, aching with overflowing urtications,
unsoothed, still, yet, still – less stable,
filled, full, flowed-over with cicatrix illustrations.

THURSDAY

Daisy Trails

Being called into the Boss' office, this Friday, was nerve-racking as usual, but not concerning. Nervously she smoothed her dress down as she entered the glass 'goldfish bowl' of Selina's outer office. Selina called her through into the main office, and waved casually at a seat, as she crossed some 't's on important papers.

Decisively she closed the papers, put them to one side, looked up and spoke breezily, not quite warmly, but certainly not coldly.

"Hello Daisy."

No one was in doubt as to who the boss was, yet the formality was easy. They had worked together for many years, and had respect and, even, some affection for one another. They spoke plainly in private.

"I'll put you out of your misery. It's good news. Better, even, than we might have thought. We start on Monday."

"Oh that's great," Daisy tried to keep some excitement out of her voice, "and is it a full-spectrum clearance?"

"I had to pull some mighty big strings, but yes it is. I know you think a month is required for enough data, but we only got a fortnight. But I also managed to get a one-week white period. Are you sure that is necessary?"

"Yes Selina, I really think so. To fully engage with the certainty that any alterations are pure, it is essential. Thank you so much, it has been years."

"Yes," replied Selina, "But I believe in this. And you."

Daisy allowed herself a smile. Yes. So she should. The concept is solid, genius even. The formula is perfect. And this weekend every airplane around the world will be having their internal tanks filled with *her* plan, *her* chemicals. For two full weeks every streak you see in the sky will be one of Daisy's trails.

There was going to be a *lot* of work to be done, in the next weeks, months, maybe years, making sense of all the data. Yes. A good Friday, literally. A shame she could tell no-one.

Viable Creations

Sitting across the table, the mustard yellow table cloth fluttering in the warm breeze, he felt he had hit upon the solution. The problem was complex, the desired outcome ambiguous, every path to a resolution tried, unclear and blocked. He, they, had thought of so many possibilities, but none quite fitted the agreement. Of course, he reasoned, why do we not simply violate the agreement (again). She was happy with this idea, except the knowledge that it would be discovered, and there would be consequences. And she, they, did not like consequences touching *them* at all. Not at all.

The limes lay, cut, on the board in the kitchen, as she gently placed the water they lightly flavoured on the table. Leaving the kitchen, entering the world, she looked breath-taking. Her ice white sarong moved as effortlessly as she did, the force of her small steps and the wind in harmony. He gasped, he could not help himself.

"Your hair looks nice today," he said, miserly in his praise. *Today* suggesting it was normally quite foul. She did not notice, either the compliment nor the implied criticism. They were happy.

Sky and sea, both blue, but so very different. A brightness in both, a depth in one. He looked up at her again and motioned. She started to pour the delicately limed water, he asked for ice. She remained sitting.

She wondered aloud what his plan was now, how to get around this awkward impasse they are stuck with, still. She groaned when she heard his response.

"Lie."

The Call of the Child

"Mum!"

Never a moment's peace. The wonders of motherhood. The pressure to be in constant awe of your child, and your own, remarkable inner sense of calm and fulfilment, that they bring.

Except they don't.

A long sigh. "WHAT?"

Irritable, always irritable. Poor little bastard. Try again.

"What? What is it, my little darling?" I wonder if children this young can hear the insincerity. If they can, what awful problems are being stored up for their future? Children are precious, adults dispensable, it seems. Yet one is just the other, the difference is only time. Why do people put such store by time? History is not sacred; it is just what happened.

But time does pass. The child does grow. The familiarity of being together, on top of each other, all these years, breeds the usual things. Contempt, certainly, but also some kind of affection. Like Stockholm Syndrome, perhaps. Is the contempt mutual? Possibly. It certainly appears to be, and to grow with time.

Angrier and angrier the child gets, until an adult it is that storms from the house. A flurry of fury and bitter words in their wake. The self-loathing of the one left behind, when they feel that most awful of emotions wash over them. Relief.

****

The child is alone. A small bed, in a small room, in a small shared flat. Things are not as they thought they might be. A strange need arises within, not material, yes they are hungry, but that's not it. Just the voice, not kind, but at least instructing, ordering, *caring*. They had not expected that. Pride, of course, stops a call being made, in person or even by telephone. Not even a text.

*   *   *   *

Far away across the teeming city, teeming with people, teeming with hopes, disappointments and despair, lies a woman, an older woman now. Longing now to hear that which she once longed so desperately to stop.

The call of the child.

Stranded in Burma

Hands shaking, head cracking, bones creaking, vomit rising, ears bleeding, now, this is now. Movement, always movement. Striding, stumbling, wading, waddling, wandering, wondering. After the movement, the mystery. Why, how, what, always, when, where, who, not so much.

I stand, here I stand, I do not move, I block out thought. Still movement, all around, a dog idles by, a cyclist zips past, clouds rush onwards, here comes the storm, rain falls, lightning rips through the sky. And I? I stand. Here I stand. Nowhere to go, no one to tell, nothing in my hands.

Drenched, I stand, I breathe, I hold out my arms. I am here, here I stand.

*   *   *   *

Later

Yes, I move, I walk, I am walking through streets of Nay Pyi Taw, you wonder, as I wander. Why am I here? When did I come? What am I doing? What have I done? What will I do? Why am I stuck? Here. Here I am.

my an mar

The Apples of Wrath

He was from Kiev, the man I met on the funicular railway. It suddenly seemed such a long way away, to him and to me. His air was that of a man not yet defeated, not fully. He sighed and sunk a tiny bit more upon learning the distance from Mersch to Hollenfels. I, in providing this information, I felt as a cold assassin must feel, slightly.

From his distant starting point, 'in Ukraine', he clarified, in the manner of one giving a present, he was heading for Hollenfels, you see. It seemed imperative that I should discover the nub of this enigma, yet his confused statements became a little more closed, on each attempt.

We spoke a mixture of his terrible English and a worse French. We appeared to be locked in a desperate need to murder the French language more fully and more rapidly than one another. It was as if our very lives depended on it; should one of us leave a breath of life in French, perhaps, we would be condemned ourselves. These linguistic dilapidations left us further confused and diminished. I suggest freely that on his part this was somewhat deliberate.

Once again I was struck by something being out of kilt. A man smoking, without cigarettes. An assumption of something hidden, hidden beneath an elderly, benign exterior. He left, I pointed him to platform one, he had fifteen minutes to wait for his train north, his destiny, maybe? My train pulled out a few moments later.

I never saw the man from Kiev again, and I never learned of his purpose. The apple crop in the north that year, however, was devastatingly disappointing.

Senseless and Staggering

The only loss that he could sustain was, perversely, the hardest loss of all.

In all moments he felt himself lost, suffocated, destroyed. Yet when the deepest trouble hit him, he was not shattered. He came into his own.

Firm, he was, and unwavering. 'Dead to me' was a phrase on his lips often, but always meant, and always faithful.

So many people gone from his life. His loyalty to himself was deep, and true and understandable, but who was the loser?

Half of nothing is nothing.

Can you not understand that once it's gone, it's gone. There is nothing left, why would there be any reason to cease? Is it just revenge? Or simply desperation? No, not desperation, more like a lack. It lacks.

Lacking in everything, a past, a future, a present. How to move forward.

"I am nothing. I have always been nothing. I cannot want to be something."

Work hard to improve. Nothing improved is still nothing.

And why? It's all senseless, a staggeringly childish fantasy.

It's all bullshit.

Splitting Threads

The dark dog ran across the beach of the tidal river, a low short patch of black shiny mud. Gradually the waters receded; lapping gently away to reveal first the feet and legs, eventually the torso.

[split – thread one] During the fearsome row the dog must have got away. Each assumed it was with the other. As their divorce grew ever more acrimonious they didn't meet again for years. In all the contacts via solicitors and courts they never once mentioned it. When finally they met, on the street, and spoke (the bitter hatred now dulled) it emerged that neither had the dog. They had no idea what had happened to it since that fateful day and they had no idea of its role in the discovery of the gangster's body.

[split – thread two] It was too big. In every sense it was too big. How on earth had they got themselves into this? Accidentally killing this Mr. Big character, they were in big, big trouble. The whole of the City's underworld would be in uproar. But first they had another big problem. He was *big*. They needed to lose the corpse, and quickly.

Although three of them were involved, that was not enough to shift him. So, more people were needed, creating yet greater risk. And transport. They had an hour until high tide, they needed to get him in the river quick. It was dark. That they were not seen manhandling him over the balustrade of the old bridge they could not believe. What they will eventually know, in time, is that they *were* seen. And that enormous splash was heard up and down the old river. The first of many, in the days and weeks to come.

Skinamarinky Dinky Dink

A fast moving fun family board game for two to eight players.

Roll Up! Roll Up! All The Fun of The Fair. The thrill and excitement of timeless travelling funfairs are captured as you travel around the board – meticulously based on Luxembourg's 700 year old *Schueberfouer* – jumping from ride to ride, trying your luck at the stalls, eating over-sugared treats as you race your competitors at that age-old funfair magic: Your money disappears before your very eyes!

Rules

Each player choses a counter and places it on the 'home' square. Deal out 50 €uros to each player. The youngest goes first. Before setting off for the fair you must first 'pester you parents' to give you money and let you go. To head off to the fair you must first roll a six. On each turn that you roll a 1, however, you receive an extra 10 €uros from Granny.

The first player to roll a 6 jumps on the tram square to get to the *Schueberfouer* – but bad luck! The tram is free now and you can't spend any money here!

Upon reaching the fair you must first choose a card, either a 'rides' card, a 'stalls' card, or a 'food' card. Inspect the card, and decided whether you wish to travel directly to the destination on it, and spend money on partaking this particular hedonism.

Rides: Each player must check the ride score against their 'fear-factor'. If it is higher, then a die must be rolled to see whether you can 'pluck up the courage' this time!

Stalls: The easiest way to lose money, whether it is hook-a-duck, the shooting range, or the Teddy Bear Raffle! But beware! Your luck may be in and these stalls *actually do pay out to winners*!!

Food: How many doughnuts, toffee apples, and chips can *you* eat before you get queasy and throw-up on a ride? Keep careful notes of your 'barf-bonus' points!!

Play continues to the left. Visit as many different sections as you can.

The Winner

The first player to spend all their money is declared the winner, and can get on with enjoying their lives once again.

Fact or Fiction

"Fifteen?"

"No. Fifty. *Fifty*. Five – oh, can you believe? In fact, our fifteen year old bab-, our teenage babysitters wouldn't even do that."

"Well, sure? They might."

"I guess, anyway, I was livid, you can imagine. I mean how can you live with yourself, how can you sleep at night?"

"I know, it is appalling, did you say anything?"

"No. Well … no."

"Well, you should, you really should. Have you seen this? I saw it earlier, hang on, I'll look for it. They put one through our door, through everyone's door, I guess. I hope anyway, maybe. Maybe just ours. Imagine if they had."

"Oh, yes, very … interesting. Odd. Did I tell you about the yellow bucket? They wanted one up at the school, I asked 'Does it *have to* be yellow?' and the answer, you can imagine, was at best inconclusive, so I called and the receptionist refused to put me through – you know the one – and so I said, 'Its a fucking bucket, alright? It's orange and the fuck's up with that?' and she got all croaky and hung up, so I don't know what I'm going to do? I'll just send her in with that one, I guess."

"Just send her in with that one."

****

The kitchen fell quiet for now, and the silence was only interrupted, gradually, as the kettle rose to a boil. The short reprieve of a sigh before it climaxed in a frenzy of noise and steam.

"Another cuppa?"

She did not look, or wait for a reply, she made it already. Opening a box of Jaffa Cakes they each took only one.

****

Dynamics of Destined Duos

There is no beginning; there is no end.

A start, of course, there must be, even if it is not the beginning. And at the start there was (is?) a body. Not just any body. The sacred body of a nobody. But before we start at this ending, we need to drop yet further back; I am, you see, determined to take a linear approach to this.

So further back, to before the body *was* a body, we go. Not to when it was a living, moving, individual, but further back, before it was even this. The atoms were around, of course, just not in this configuration.

So this takes us to two bodies. Their attraction so strong it is able to conjure up, out of nothing, yet more bodies. Not a skill to be sniffed at, you'd think, yet, hardly a head is turned at these events.

All around the globe there are duos dancing this amazing creation, and all around the globe are long existant atoms forging together to create the wonderous, multiple, ordinary, uniqueness that is life, and all over the globe are these being shattered, torn apart and once more returned to the universe, to form yet new entities, sentient or non-sentient.

Which brings us back to our body. The miracle of millions of years of refining, a perfect, complex object capable of extraordinary feats, both every-day wonders and one-off breakthroughs. Truly inspiring and astounding.

The dynamics of the duo are required to bring this all together, but only one, oneself, required to expire.

The Stop (but not The End)

Simpleminded Twists

She woke up – and it was all a dream. She caught her breath, and sighed a long sigh of relief. What an awful dream, it may well have been in self-defence, but killing that man and the long-winded attempts to hide his body. Well, it was just *awful*.

Rising and entering the kitchen she put the coffee on, and searched in the bread-bin. The only result was a couple of old slices of stale white, so she shrugged and popped them in the toaster.

It was then that she saw him lunge at her. Panicked, what the fuck is someone doing in *my* kitchen, he grabbed her by the neck as she involuntarily moved back. He held her hard, but only had one arm pinned, the other flailed around, hitting the work surface. Hardly noticing what it was, her hand rested on the big vegetable knife. Reader, she stabbed him.

He staggered back, releasing her and clutching at the back of his neck. He could not reach the knife, buried so deeply, and nor did he have enough time, for his life was already at an end. She half screamed, and panted, yet it only took her a few moments to recover.

Now comes the tricky part, she thought, remembering the dream of last night. First, she figured, clean up the mess. The noise as she pulled the knife out was unexpected. A little like driving a wooden tent peg into an over-ripe melon, but in reverse. She cleaned that up and then started on the blood. So much blood.

[author's note: the alarm goes off at this juncture, signalling the end of my ten minutes. Damn, I was just getting started. Now, I need to tie

this up somehow, nicely., and with a twist. Alarm, eh? Ah yes, an
alarm]

BEEP-BEEEP. Her alarm went off, crashing into the quiet morning. She woke up – and it was all a dream (again).

Toilet Paper Testimonies

And that is how I ended up in Radio Krakow.

But before we get there, just now, we need to head back a few hours. Well maybe longer, a few days, back when we first saw that extraordinary achievement, whilst *leaving* Krakow. It had been a grand few days; coming on top of several awful months.

That had started, in fact, in the very height of the summer, yet here we are now depths of winter, the snow, of course, is what had drawn us here. I will not talk, not here, of what had happened in the summer. That is for another place. It is important, however, to understand what happened on that crisp January day: to have a picture of what had been going on all those months.

Stress. A variety of stresses bearing down, with a variety of outcomes. Difficulty of thought, difficulties all round: a sudden, and somewhat dramatic, weight-loss as food exited the sphere of consciousness. In all honesty consciousness itself had pretty much absented the stage too. So here we are. In southern Poland, diminished in size.

Alas! A reawakening, a (dare we say?) recovery, of sorts, led to renewed consumption. A sudden, and somewhat dramatic, rediscovery of food. Joy, and happiness all around. Well, not quite, not by a long chalk, but a few square meals at any rate. Sustenance, of a physical nature.

The day beckoned, rather, in retrospect I suppose we could say that it loomed.

A solid and terrible vow has been made, under the most ancient available oak tree, at the usual appointed hour (midnight), by all involved, a vow of silence. Certainly the good people of Radio Krakow, and I myself, will never speak of what went on in there. But rest assured, the children of their toilet paper suppliers will enjoy an extraordinary Christmas this year.

Partly Paisley

Jim and Dave often met at the pub. They usually sat at the same table, but it wasn't important to them. Today, as it happens, they were. Dave had bought this round, but now they were comfortably into their pints, not far but a while until they finished. This was what they came for. A time to sit and sip, a time to relax and chat.

Equally comfortable were their silences. Old, old friends and colleagues, they enjoyed each other's outlook and insights, but were close enough to just sit.

Right now, however, they were laughing. Jim's deadpan delivery of the news regarding one of their old, hated, bosses left Dave full of joy. The tears ran down both their faces, as they clutched themselves and gradually regained composure, still punctuated by the odd chuckle.

Simon had finally come-a-cropper. His self-important arrogance, which when coupled with his incompetence had made him such an awful manager, had at long last been his undoing.

Jim had heard it on the grapevine. How they both longed to have been there to see it with their own eyes.

Misty Morning Melancholy

Wake. Eyes open slowly, what is this? Oh yes. The familiar room, the familiar feeling. Not this again. Body slumped across the bed, warm and unfeeling. Necessity demands you move. Quitting the vertical comfort is hard enough. Face the day. Christ, not *another* one? When will it end?

Draw the curtains. Visibility poor, like losing your glasses and peering at a Monet from afar in poor light. What fresh horrors today?

Socks. How many millions of times? It seems that pulling on socks must constitute a significant portion of life. It is a tiresome and annoying task. When will it end? This infernal socking of the part of you that is so distant, the furthest from 'you'. What is 'you'?

Sit on the bed. Half-socked. What is this all? View the day ahead? What is the point of any of it? Time passes. The alarm repeats. Now late, the morning is already taking a turn for the worse. Urgent cajoling needed now, no time for coffee. The clock is the vicious gang-master of the morning. Every single second already spent and however frugal you are, there is never quite enough.

Breakfast eaten. Breaking a fast; this should be a joyful time, like sunset during Ramadan, as cities come back to life. But no. Shovel it in. Bland, uninteresting, worthy. And now. Stomach uneasily groaning under the enforced strain, you leave.

Into the mist. The warm enveloping embrace of a cold melancholy. Another fucking day.

The Widow's Web

Pushing back a tiny plate, displaying no more than a smear of a crumb, she sank herself down in her chair. Delicate, translucent and unmoving, few would even notice that the cavernous armchair held anything more than a bundle of blankets. She breathed, but it could not been seen nor heard.

Preserving all, every drop, of her energy internally, not a single speck was wasted on physical movement. Her eyes, even, whilst alert, remained cloudy and motionless. She did not look, nor did she expend a calorie in closing the eyelids. She thought.

All around her, through the forest and across to the great city, in stark contrast, the action was frenzied. Deals being done, bones being broken, acquisitions being made. Carefully the threads were loosened, untangled, removed. No one would ever consider, perhaps, that all those myriad nefarious dealings had but a single source. And should they, well, tracing it to that source, out here, is impossible. Impossible to achieve, impossible to believe.

To have been that careful, for that long, a whole lifetime, is enough, dear reader, to tell you what a remarkable creature we have encountered here. Not one risk, not one chance, not one mistake, across all those decades. Even as her beloved partner found himself in fatal trouble, trouble that she could have solved with no more than a couple of nods in the right direction, she feared it being the means of her discovery. So, she remained unmoved, unmoving.

Decades of loneliness and misery may indeed have followed, but also decades of further success. Not one thing happened for one hundred miles around that armchair without her say-so, without her cut. Regrets? Not a single one. Even as she thought to herself, all those years ago, there was not a shred of doubt or concern.

"I'll not lift a single bony finger to help him."

The Hipster Hygienist

That beard is a problem, right from the off. It's got egg in it. The white coat doesn't convince anyone. There are braces underneath, for sure. Rinsing your mouth in a craft beer fails to refresh the mouth, or the breath. The retro equipment is somewhat off-putting, you really just want the most modern assistance to painless dentistry available.

After knocking off, he hangs up the coat and dons the Tweed. Perfect skin, smooth fingers, what in his life requires those heavy hob-nailed boots? Stopping on the way home for a cup of his preferred brew he is appalled to find that the wrong grade of blade has been used on the beans. He splutters it out, coffee splashing across the floor, this young-old man finds himself with a face of rage, on a Friday night.

Yorkshire Pudding People

Norfolk Dumplings, atop a warm rich stew
Lancashire Hotpot, for cold rainy nights.
Cumberland Sausage, curled like a screw,
Chelsea Buns, rich cinnamon bites.

Cornish Pasties, handy to carry,
Bedfordshire Clanger, almost its equal.
Staffordshire Oat Cakes, lovely with cherry,
Yorkshire Pudding, let's eat, come on people.

FRIDAY

Dimly Lit Distractions

Jonathan Pixie Nickleby skipped through the forest, he hoped to see his friends. He knocked at Crealy Bealy's front door, but the rabbit was not at home. On he skipped. He whistled to himself (a cheery tune). He arrived at the house of Alastair Bear, the biggest pig of all.

"What a huge door," Jonathan Pixie Nickleby thought to himself, "What a GIGANTIC house." He tapped his tiny knuckle on the massive, thick wooden door.

No answer here, either, so he checked next-door to see if Alastair Bear's best friend, Cedric Anglestone Whoop McGraw was in. He gently tickled the door with just one figure, it was so small he could hardly see it. Sadly, even this light touch was enough to knock it off its miniscule hinges, for Cedric Anglestone Whoop McGraw was the tiniest mouse in all of Figpaddle Wood.

"Where *is* everyone today?" wondered Jonathan Pixie Nickleby, out loud.

"THEY ARE AT PING POND." declared The Voice, that booms around Figpaddle Wood from time to time. Off Jonathan Pixie Nickleby trotted, as fast as his little legs would carry him, off to Ping Pond.

When he arrived, what a sight he saw! All his friends around Ping Pond, staring at a ginormous yacht. There was Crealy Bealy. There was Cedric Anglestone Whoop McGraw. And there was Alastair Bear, eyeing up the boat longingly.

Fifty Shades of Embarrassment

Peeling away from the group, Edward began to get a little hot under the collar. Except in extreme circumstances, he really could not stand to be in a group of people of any size, well, not even of one. Travis had shouted out at him, and tried to make him welcome, and bring him into the group. Edward knew then that Travis must die. Regretfully, he needed to solve yet another problem, he derived no pleasure, and a lot of misery, from these situations.

Cursing to himself over his ill-luck, Edward started to think about a plan. Last time he was very nearly found out, the dog was the weak link in *that* plan. Although he had a preferred method of dispatch for those needing to be silenced, he recognised the need to strike in a different manner each time. Relax, he thought, this is a cracker. Kneeling in the mud he carefully slipped a coat hanger in the gap of the door. Easing the car door open was a doddle, now to track his prey.

Inside the car, he kept low and drove slowly, around and around the building where the party was taking place. Soon enough, Travis emerged, a little the worse for wear, and stumbling along the road.

Accelerating hard, the bonnet of the car hit the back of Travis' legs, and his upper body was thrown in the air, and flung away from the car, near lifeless already.

Car accidents are so ubiquitous, nobody questions the motives. Unending carnage is considered normal and acceptable. Nobody truly questions the driver. There but for the Grace of God, they think, go I, and there went Edward, free and calm.

Juggling Julie

Awake at six am, two minutes to breathe. Then it begins.

Up and into the kitchen, kettle on, bowls and spoons out, get cereal and juice ready. Shout up to the kids, quick shower, out, and now really cajole the kids down to eat.

Play a game – 'Who can get dressed the quickest?' – how much longer will they still fall for *that*?

Out the door, walk the kids to the school gates, remind one about P.E. and assure the other you'll be there for the concert at lunchtime.

Run to bus, panic at traffic, get to work on time – just. Manager gives you a look. Please God, no call from the teacher *today*.

No lunch, but manic running around means you see the show (*The* definitive guide to parenting: 'Be There'). Back to work.

Boss being an insufferable bore, as usual, but today you must get those reports done, no avoiding that. Working hard all afternoon but still finish late. Hurried call *again*.

Reports finally done (manager long gone) rush to sister's flat to get the kids. Usual craven gratitude to a sister who says it is 'a pleasure' (and actually, means it) but this does not resolve your guilt and self-loathing for letting her, and your kids, down. Again.

Stop at shops to get stuff for your mum, kids complaining, stop at mums you have to take a tea, guilty you stayed so long, guilty you could not stay longer.

Tea for the kids, bath and bedtime, find the energy from somewhere to read a story, you all three love it, but it is exhausting and your head nods while you read. Guilt again. 'Do the voices, mummy.'

Cinema at the weekend, and swimming too, if you forego your Friday night bottle of wine, a small price to see their joyful wet faces.

Julie has been juggling life since the man she thought she knew, and knew she loved, turned out to know he did not love her, and was not who she thought she knew, but a selfish, childish, cunt.

Suffocated in Sinopia

Deep inside the rainbow is joy, an uplifting and life-affirming happiness that trips along through the sky. As the hues change, the feeling is refreshed anew with vibrancy. The spectrum holds distinct colours, it is true, and the infinite variety between, creates myriad moods of positivity.

I, however, I am stuck. The rainbow, and its cousins across the full palette are but a distant aspiration, a haunting half memory, strong enough to entice, too weak to enrich.

No, not all, it is not fair to say all. I am stuck in a certain area of this rich tapestry of colour, and it would be wholly unfair to describe the browns as any lesser than any other region. Indeed the deep, strong, mellow and gentle shades of brown are, of themselves, a remarkable place to be.

But I, I am stuck. In a single tiny spot. Again it is a delightful spot, if one were to pass through, or even to linger, but to stay? Stay put for all eternity. It is suffocating me. Its natural warmth, a boon to most, begins to pall after a long period of time. And by now I am quite, quite mad. I think. How can I know, when all I see, smell, feel, hear and taste is this one precise colour? You should try it. Help.

203, 65, 11

Billowy Blobs and Booby Traps

He still believes. It is not so much he believes that the good times will return; rather that these are *still* the good times. Presumably to get yourself out every show, to an ever diminishing audience, you need this denial. The venues getting smaller, the towns getting more undistinguished, the memory of the act less tangible.

Ten years on the telly. Somehow that seems to translate into a blink of an eye for most people, unless you happened to be the exact right age to have grown up with the gentle puppets, Billowy and Booby. But for most people it's a minor quiz question, getting harder as every year passes; "How were Mr. Blobs and Mr. Traps better known?"

So, for their operator, and his rather uncomfortable screen presence they are still very real and very relevant, his only chance of an income. Those young enough to remember the show are now at an age where they are past the first nostalgia for their early years, and a long way off living exclusively in the past. They are too busy living to think about going to see this half-remembered has-been. He, meanwhile, is caught in the no-man's land of ex-TV stars, where news of his death will be greeted by the words, "Oh, is he still alive?"

But for now he has a performance to give, a few dozen people not quite sure who he or his frayed and battered companions are.

And just like his beloved puppets, he is not dead; but not quite living.

Delirious Intentions

So the circle is broken. But it is still a unit, of sorts. There is a double knot at the bottom, and a line from these up to one, on the right, and another up to the left. And this is where the problem lies.

The intentions are insane. It batters away from the outside, constantly trying to smash and break this unit. A cuckoo in the nest, bewildered and angry that this is not encouraged from the other strand. How can it be? Why would it be?

Coming off from the outside on the left is another strand. This is it, dark and destructive, but bizarrely encouraged from that side. To ruin what is left.

*   *   *   *

I dreamt, last night, that I was still on the aeroplane. I had in my hands some string. It wound around my hands and I could not stop looking at the threads. Eventually my eyes – my dreameyes – followed the threads outwards, and it was clear. This string roved throughout the 'plane, and it had access all areas. Two special holes in the flight deck door allowed it in and out, and around and around it went before returning, seamlessly, back to me.

I was in the back row. I was serene. I was sitting in an aisle seat. The 'plane landed.

*   *   *   *

Why? Why the fuck *should* I raise a single finger to aid the destruction of the unit. The knots are too precious. And this outside force must, will, be stopped.

103

Wednesday's with Mary

Eight kids would seem, perhaps, one too many. Of course she was exhausted, who wouldn't be? To have done it within a decade too. What a time that was! Constantly pregnant, babies everywhere, ever more mouths to feed. More help though, too, as they got older. Neither of them would have it any other way, though. A houseful indeed, but a house full of life and love.

She knew, right from the off, him too. They both wanted a large family. Using the unusual name 'Monday' for the first child, a beautiful bundle of joy she still recalled that (first) magical moment even now, was a marker. A statement of intent. By the time Tuesday came along, within *ten months* of Monday it was clear that the names would run out before her desire for children would. And besides that, the third child, the second girl, just did not *look* like a 'Wednesday'. So Mary she was.

Oddly the skipped day continued, the fourth became Thursday and on and on, until Sunday, and then the last. They knew it was the last, just as they had known there would be many more than one. They could just tell. And now they are growing up, Monday already at University, the noise was beginning to fade. She wasn't sure, truly, if she was ready for that just yet, though. Life will be so dull.

When the eighth was born it was clear. Her deep, deep brown eyes, her dark, black hair. That look of hers; "Here I am: deal with it." Yes this was her 'Wednesday' alright. No mistake.

Sitting here, this afternoon, on her own, most of the kids at school, Wednesday with Mary, she reflected. Reflected on an exhausting, difficult, insanely challenging life. She thought of each of her five girls and three boys, each so very different, each so very wonderful. She reflected happily, a little moment for a rest at last.

Ah yes. A life worth living.

Circle In The Sky

Dreaded shapes hurtling around, losing our form. When you cannot tell where the shape-seller ends and the world begins, you know things are beginning to fail. The gentle fizzling out of their being, something around the hair, it is impossible to determine where they cease, where their edge is. Do they have an edge?

Looking up there is no cloud. Invisibly, maybe the moisture is held, suspended. Blue, such a vibrant blue, searing through the whole vista. Look up, look up! When did you last look up? To see such vastness, it is always there, remember to look up. Here in these flatlands it is enormous, human eyes insufficient to take in the entirety of the three hundred and sixty degrees of the horizon and the magnificent dome above.

They are running out; circles all gone, rhomboids too. You settle on a square, although the price is noticeably greater than the less precise rectangle. Shuffling slowly along the queue you see the few remaining shapes leave with grim-faced, determined, satisfied shoppers, stomping slowly off with their shapes paid for and wrapped. So few remain.

Finally you reach the front. There is a single square left, you request it. Handing over a filthy, well-handled, greasy note leads the shape-seller to wrinkle their nose in disdain. As they hand you over the final square you sense a deep misery descend on those behind you in the queue.

"And here's your change: back to you". A rattle of coins in your upstretched hands. You turn and leave.

Presumed Guilty

The child sat motionless in the chair, behind the desk. It was their typical seat, third row back, toward the right. The lesson had been, also typically, a little unruly, the teacher sighing as yet another class was not quite in her control. It always felt, still, a little haphazard; she was clinging on by her fingertips. The target knowledge always felt undelivered.

In the noise, chaos, and desperate attempts to fulfil a role just out of her reach, she barely noticed him. A quiet student was, to be honest, a relief. It was not a pupil she saw there, rather a hole that didn't need filling, didn't need her attention.

So week after week he sat, motionless. Not studious, but apparently attentive. Then around half way through her second year with this class, he continued this motionless state after the bell had gone, along with it his classmates in a untidy and uncontrolled exit.

She looked up and began to call his name, and realised she couldn't remember it. "I am", she thought, depressingly, "a failing teacher."

A quick glance in her book and the name came back to her. Still he didn't respond. She approached him. He was dead.

* * * *

The subsequent investigations, that she carried out into his class-mates, suggested to one and all that she, herself, was in fact guilty. She was tried and went down, finally free from the tyranny of her own failing classroom.

* * * *

It was many, many, years later and she was still doing time, when it was discovered, this special form of suicide. His hidden writings, found when his parents finally gave up the misery of life without an only child, and the house was sold. The teacher was presumed guilty, but in fact he had chosen to bore himself to death. He finally achieved this difficult endeavour in one of her – oh so very, very, dull – lessons.

Yet now she is presumed innocent, perhaps.

Foolish Incantation

Welcome aboard this Airline flight today. Please pay careful attention to the following safety instructions:

Please make sure that your hand luggage is securely stowed under the seat in front of you or in the overhead bin.

This aircraft has four emergency exits, all marked with 'EXIT'-signs: two in the front, and two in the rear. Please locate your nearest exit, which may be situated behind you.

Emergency lights on the floor show you the way to the emergency exits. Fasten your seatbelt whenever the 'Fasten seatbelt' sign is on. The belt is closed and opened like this. For your own safety we advise you to keep your seatbelt fastened while seated.

In case of loss of cabin pressure, oxygen masks will be automatically released above your seats. Pull down the nearest mask, place it over mouth and nose and secure it with the elastic band. If travelling with children please secure your own mask before assisting them.

Your life vest is located under your seat. In the event of landing on water, place the life vest over your head, fasten the straps at the front of the vest and pull them tight. Do not inflate the vest inside the aircraft. As you leave the aircraft, pull down the red tabs to inflate the vest. If necessary the life vest can be inflated by blowing through these tubes.

We hope you enjoy your flight.

Illegally Brunette

Let's be honest, it is more a crime of geography than anything else. The argument was always thin for the segregation, only provided as an excuse for those who wanted it already. For other reasons. In each of the zones stylists naturally specialised, it could not really be helped. Fashions change, however, and of course a certain type of person, at a certain type of age, will always want to shock.

There was nothing, anyway, in any pamphlet, or constitution, that mentioned dyes, of course. Not yet. It was not very easy to find someone willing to do it, although not very difficult either. It was frowned upon, rather than anything stronger. And once the craze hit, the entire industry became a charged one, old friends, partners, all divided neatly into those that dyed and those that didn't.

No one could really get why that one post on BlondBook made such a stir. Soon viral, and from the initial shock, repulsion even, came some copycats. These early ones wanted to cash in on a bit of the rebellion kudos, but it was amazing how quickly it became mainstream. This is when the problems began; when people started to see the inherent beauty in it.

This led to wider debates, and the once niche ProAllHair group started to gain support, not only across society, but across *societies*, and cross hair border meetings intensified. Obviously the authorities had to act. What started with a simple ban on dye ended, not so very long after, with many deaths.

A salutary lesson in there, somewhere.

Creator of Days
"What are days? Days are where we live."
Philip Larkin – Days

This is morning. It crawls in, in a fog that clears as awareness overcomes, in stages, perhaps. Who makes my days now? Not I, I think, although the uncontrolled hyperactivity within my skull must take some blame. Yet, it is morning, during this process of emerging into our conscious state, that it is calmed, mostly, at least for a few seconds. First comes light.

Or is the light first? I am here, just, fumbling for who I am, where I am. The primal and modern human interact as this basic state has a need imposed upon it. Time. What is the time? A host of modern devices provide this information – the sun, or lack of, is just broad strokes – and by the time it has all registered, the horror of day ahead is rebounding around and around my head.

Recently the day has been so hard to face, removing oneself from bed has been almost too great a hurdle. Staying in bed, also unthinkably grim. A no-man's land briefly, safe in here. Not safe, but the day's failures do not commence until the first foot hits the floor. Unless … unless this takes too long, then the failure starts prostrate.

Who is the creator of these days? Not I. One far away who is never far from my thoughts. He has created this monster that I am failing to live with. He, whose days are full of weightless structure, of contentedness punctuated with sparks of happiness. A scale, a direct correlation.

My days are misery, unstructured and full of sparks of desolation, sparks that sting, and form my days. Created of cruelty.

The Sugar Coated Nutsack

"I can't sugar-coat this, I'm afraid", the doctor stated, alarmingly, "It is not good news."

Hector swallowed hard. He hadn't even wanted to go that day, although he would never have imagined the eventual reason to avoid going. He just usually found it dull. In the end, on this occasion, it was anything but dull.

Nothing appeared amiss when they knocked on the door. It creaked open and he remembers – how oh innocent then! – giggling to himself and thinking that was so clichéd, if this were a horror movie. Which is wasn't, this was life. The frail and gentle old lady behind the door not only put his mind at rest, but also gave him that surge of excitement he had forgotten about.

Here was the easiest of easy marks.

Or so they thought.

It may have been hours, it may even have been days ago, Hector thought as he lay in the hospital. They gained entrance well enough, and started the patter happily. She seemed attentive and responsive. And gull-i-ble. Before they knew what was happening, she was giving them the tour of her modest home. Including the cellar.

Ah. The cellar.

They were found on the street, knocked out, and riddled with pain which got worse as their consciousness increased. The scoring and burning all over their skin was horrendous. Evidence of extreme temperatures, of hot oil and worse, was everywhere. Sugar melts at 186 degrees Celsius. That *is* hot.

"Yes, I'm afraid it is completely covered. It will be *extremely* painful removing it, and then the burns below. Uff. It will be a long, slow, and painful process, I'm afraid. It'll be a while before you are going door-to-door again, I'm sorry."

The doctor was kindly, but you could tell he wasn't keen on their shady way of making a living. He hadn't been noticeably gentle so far. He, like the police, didn't believe their story for one second.

She was, after all, such a sweet old lady.

In The Midst Of Sadness and Despair

Calm now. A calmness surrounds, for the most part. And each time it descends it seems it is over. A corner turned. Then something brings it out again, a date, an event, a location, a memory, a thought. And once more stepping into the sadness and despair, the soul emptying misery that is a persistent companion.

For now, though, in the midst of this sadness and despair, a moment of calm. And yes. The storm seems to be abating, slowly and with many heavy squalls still. The bubble is delicate, but it weathers the day-to-day, puncturing only on the fierce spike of reality. And suddenly surrounded at these moments once more, like a dense, crushing cloud. Maybe it is a room, a round room. It spins and there is no way out, and no way forward, and no way to control anything.

The round room, yes that is it. In its midst there is a hopelessness: a grim grey space where hope should be. Yet hope? Does hope help, can it assist in protection from the sadness and despair? No, hope merely feeds it; it is air flowing onto to a fire just as the never-changing hurt is the fuel.

Invincible Endeavours

Flying through the night Bernard found his thoughts turning to the seat beside him. How fortunate, he had thought, to have a spare seat alongside him on such a busy flight. He settled down to read and relax and tensed only slightly during the intense acceleration of take-off.

Levelling off he began to feel uncomfortable however. There was a sense of discomfort. Something was wrong. The engine noise was loud, but he felt a gentle, regular sound underneath. He was sure it was breathing, but probably his own. He held it and counted to ten. No, it was still there.

His arm slipped off the armrest. Slipped, or pushed? Bernard dare not think about this or make any other attempts to see what was in this seat beside him.

The window shade lowered itself.

The Brat in the Hat

Wants, want, wanting. Where does this desire come from? If some is good, more must be better, right? Is having worse than getting? Is wanting worse than having? The glutton, the greedy, these are the great enemies, no? To have, it is immoral, of course it is. On the other hand, we must have something, food, clothes, we must have enough. Where is a line, does anyone need a hat *that* big? Does anyone need *that many* hats? When is enough too much, when is desire greed? When you have more than I? I guess.

Evidence of Greatness

Often in the never-lost lanes of the Old Town
A cat is happened upon, a feral feline
At once at home, and without a home
Lost, found, sin hogar, sin casa, sin nada.

Casi siempre en las calles (always lost), of esta
Pinche cuidad, puedes ver un hombre,
Perdido. Yes, you *can* find this man, and
He cannot know, what it is to be home elsewhere.

Is he lost? This is home, to him.
Anda, duerme, come (casi nada) aquí, always,
Underneath these stars, the electric lights
That illuminate his once-loved face, una cara
Que tiene, somewhere, escondido, evidencia de su
grandeza.

SATURDAY

A Fugitive on the Loose, Where's the Noose?

A glint from the shadows, a momentary glint of light in the darkness. A single short breath was the only reaction he allowed himself, but he was wildly aware of the increased threat.

Within the shadow, however, a bead of sweat broke out on the forehead, and snaked down the side of the face, driven by a formidable and awful power, beyond the control of the straining brain secreted below that forehead. She knew that the metal object in her hand had given away her position.

Whose move next?

This is not, however, a game that regulates on turns: they both moved. Instinctively he went down and forwards, she drew back. And like that, in half of a blink of an eye, they were off again.

At full stretch she sprinted into the darkness, the sweat now enveloping her completely, the gun's secure position in her tight grip under risk. His hurried footsteps started a beat after hers, but she heard them not, her breathing too loud, her brain focusing on 'flight' to the detriment of the senses.

She knew, her experience and intelligence told her, that they would not be merely chasing her, but they would be chasing her somewhere, a trap, a cordon of officers ready to contact like a noose. He knew where, she needed to keep moving, and all the time think, guess, second-guess.

He smiled as she ducked down the alley. His plan was working, she would emerge into his carefully constructed cage. He slowed, followed her down the alley, his people would do the job.

Emerging into the beautiful, rain-soaked, medieval square he looked. Where was she? Where was his team? What had gone wrong?

*   *   *   *

The overnight train left the ornate, majestic arch of the central station on time. The last ticket was brought in cash, sweat-stained notes thrust hurriedly across the counter.

And Completely by Mistake, the Switch was Made

This is where I come in. I was asked to cover for a sick colleague. All I had to do, they said, was stand still in a corner and watch. Which I did. The problem was, I didn't know what I was watching for. So I just watched. People mainly, coming and going, circulating in the party. It was interesting yet unengaging. Little did I expect anyone to approach me.

He was tall and unkempt, but you could see beneath it and in the voice (that voice!) that he was clearly a distinguished individual. He asked me an extraordinary question regarding an otter. Unfortunately, his accent and smooth (so smooth!) tones led me to misunderstand initially. I thought he was talking about a rotter, which I could not grasp, then I thought the subject was Ray Liotta. I dare not ask him to repeat yet again, it was becoming embarrassing, rude. Was he Ray Liotta? He could be, older of course, maybe in character for a part? I found myself staring.

"Is that a red otter?" was the repeated question. I had no idea, of course, there being no otters at all in this swanky party, I was quite sure. I knew a thing or two about otters, though, so started babbling about the number of hairs per square centimetre that they boast. This is an astonishing fact, that has never previously failed to amuse and fascinate. Not Ray (sorry, it wasn't Ray Liotta, I keep forgetting; in my mind it was, and always will have been)

I made my excuses and stuck out my hand to shake it. My temporary works badge was in my hand, I had forgotten. His eyes lit up, and he placed his hand in mine, and put his other on my shoulder. He took my badge. He slipped a gun in my jacket pocket. Why, Ray, Why?

Douglas O'Malley

Solidly, he walked along the boardwalk without finding any of the sidestreets he was hoping to slip down. The breeze was picking up and began to bite through his woollen cardigan. She had been a bit lost when she asked him for the favour, and was pleased to be able to assist in some small way.

This, of course, was what bought him on this futile trek through the city. Meanwhile, she was preparing the stalls without any idea that he was failing her. She had assumed that when he agreed to take it on, it was as good as done. His incompetence had the certainty and bulk of an African elephant, but he oozed the settled confidence of a casino owner, and this had carried him through.

Finally, he turned and trudged wearily home. Another failed project he convinced himself was a success.

The Order of Things Unseen

Of the many entrances the largest one uses, quite naturally, only the main entrance, the biggest of them all. They also enter first. Given the sudden urge to retreat underground at the first break of light each morning, and the large number in this colony, it matters who goes first.

It is true always, whichever of the setts they retire too, this rule of weight applies. The most imposing first, the slightest last. This is the case, of course, for the Common Badger but not the other, more grotesquely frightening, variety.

And one was abroad this very night. This is why there was such a scurry to retreat to the nearest den, earlier than usual, for the Puff Badger spooks even its distant cousin, the mighty, robust Common Badger.

The distinctive rustling and almost-puffing will be familiar to all who have ever spent a night outdoors in the East Anglian countryside. I am afraid a tent will not protect you, and you are best advised to hide away in something more solid, because the Puff Badger will not be deterred. They will get you. This indeed is the order of the unseen.

Panicky and Peculiar

He woke up a bit bewildered, where was he? What day was it? Ahh, well must have been one of those nights. Give it a minute, it'll come. No alarm, so either weekend or too early. He curled up and dropped off to sleep again, his head cradled upside. He was lovely and warm, it occurred to him, perhaps.

Some time later, he had no idea how much time, he stirred and stretched. Wow. I've never stretched like that before, long, languid and deep, he felt his bones creak. He wondered if it was age. How bad was last night?! Even now it was still a little distant, like trying to grasp a rainbow. It was there, but not quite.

His pyjamas were warm and fuzzy, he half-noticed. More fully he was aware of the smell of his breath: rancid. Last night, last night. Slowly an image emerged. He was hammered. Oh and yes, that bloke he was chatting to. That weird bloke. He made all sorts of claims, was he weird or was he just hilarious? It was hard to tell. No matter, it was a fun night, how had he got home? He could not remember this at all.

Oh bloody hell, I went back to his, we drank more, then, oh yes, that stupid game! He was pretending he had created some sci-fi style machine, what was it? Time travel? No. Something similar, from some book or other. He was so insistent, so convinced! That was part of the brilliance of his comedy: he was straight, dead-pan, like he really believed it.

Jeff Goldblum! Kafka! Oh yes, now he remembered they talked for hours about Metamorphosis. What a weirdo! Oh well, better get up.

Dan licked his shoulder, jumped on all fours and walked past his bedroom mirror. That is peculiar, he thought to himself, and panicked.

Squinting through Blue Sky

So today I nearly touched it. It was there, I could feel, no, see, well, anyway. A sense. A sense of clouds parting and seeing through to the blue skies. What everyone has been talking about. It made sense, it was clear, perhaps. It was so delicate though, like I did not dare look at it in case it disappeared.

It disappeared, of course. The clouds crashed back together, and a heavy storm is raging once again. But I am left with that knowledge that it might be out there after all. It was like gossamer, I could not hold or study it. It is hard to try and see through the clouds again. I worry by looking too close I will see that I was wrong. It is not blue sky. An illusion. There are more and other clouds I have simply missed. I feel, I fear, that this must be the case.

Walking back carrying the rain within my chest, the wind howling inside my head, my feet and legs made of cloying, heavy, sinking sands, I knew. This once more was a mirage, a false dawn, I can leave no cliché unturned.

Once more. Questions, cascading through my mind, do I have no answers? Only time will tell, it is said. But I know. I know the answers are held within those clouds, and time will play out as I see it, bleak and unrelenting; it is written in the clouds.

Wolleken.

Pandemonium of a New Kind

First it was the lizards. Slowly it spread through the animals, easing from one species to the next, increasing in size before reaching the great apes some weeks later, and onwards to the elephants.

The zoo turned a blind eye, the visitors did not. Despite the fear, and the scare stories, visitor numbers had never been higher. Queues round and around The Regent's Park were viewed greedily by the management, warily by the The Royal Park keeper. The alteration in the crowds came as subtly as did that of the inmates themselves. It made sense, of course, in retrospect that a change in the conditions and behaviour would lead to a change in those wanting to come and experience.

Even the General Manager began to worry about what was happening. A younger, nastier, angrier crowd. Once the preserve of young children, the majority of those packing out the zoo were now male and unsure. Eventually there came the day when not a single family ticket was sold, unprecedented in one hundred and ninety-one years.

The next major shift, the straw that broke the camel's back, was the day the anteater awoke and a new kind of pandemonium broke out; the sound of which could be heard even under the great gothic roof of St Pancras station.

Macaroni Madness

Softly the pasta plops into the simmering boil. Cheese in Bedlem. A cheese sauce, baked-in sauce, a harder cheese grated and individually added at the point of eating. Milk to drink and yoghurt for pudding. The daily dairy delights. This can't be alright, this all-white meal.

Tomatoes; peppers, lentils, salmon and ketchup, red wine to drink and strawberries for dessert. They cannot all be fed with this all-red meal.

Coloured pastas come next, green and red and black. Black pasta with squid ink and mussels. A pint of Guinness goes well with those mussels they say. Rich dark chocolate mousse to end. Followed by coffee. They say it is an aphrodisiac this all-black meal.

A brown Windsor soup to start, followed by beef with new potatoes and gravy. Crème brûlée so rich and creamy. A mug of milky tea washes it down. Cannot help but frown at this all-brown meal.

Springtime Splendour

Pulling at his earlobe the ageing bank manager considered the frontage of his bank. Standing squarely, proudly and immovable in the very heart of the town. Deep coloured bricks, an impressive and solid building, the sense that it had always been there, would always be there, was palpable. Something, however, was not quite right. A splash of colour met his affronted eyes and he hurried to open up.

Seated now, in his office, he worried and thought. Miss Perkins had arrived and was called into the inner sanctum. Standing (never, ever to sit in this room) she listened intently to his concerns. She understood, and sympathised, but of course this was outside of her purview.

Naturally the manager agreed, was slightly perturbed in fact, that she may think that he wanted her to deal with it personally. No, no, they must consider who it was they must notify. Miss Perkins felt certain it was a job for the Town Council, which in truth it probably was.

This caused all manner of confusion, however. Obviously it was not possible for the manager to take the word of Miss Perkins, he must overrule her. Certain protocols had to be observed. Secondly his extremely complex relationship with the Council clouded the issue. He felt his long held burning desire to become, one day, mayor of this small settlement was well hidden, concealed. It was not. Would a complaint, at this time, be seen as an attack, his being awkward and attempting a Machiavellian approach to his ambitions? Or would tackling the problem himself be seen as over-riding the Council's responsibilities. Tricky, very tricky indeed. He mused this problem the whole day, to the exclusion of all other business. Loans, overdrafts and repayment schedules were all put to one side whilst he tried to figure out his next move.

Meanwhile, the tiny weed continued to grow in a crack at the base of the step of his Bank.

Keeper of Her Heart

I bought my first heart in Albacete. Back then things were simpler, humidity was lower, and maintaining them caused fewer headaches.

That one was not a particularly nice one, not in good nick, but you know how it is: your first one is always special, whatever it is. I have it now, I see it there, and it transports me back in time much more vividly than any of the many I've had since.

I had to take a bus there, the train was out that weekend, and it seemed a long journey. I guess it was a long journey, even then. I stayed is a very cheap *pension* that did a great line in sleepless nights, skin complaints and cockroaches.

The next morning I organised the deal, paid the cash, and spent the rest of the day in lines at the Ayuntamiento sorting out all the paperwork. How I grew to love, and crave, the sound of the heavy stamp coming down hard on thin paper. Finally I was all done.

By now the train was running again, and so myself and my heart travelled swiftly west to Madrid, and onwards, wherever my heart desired.

It led me to you, to your heart. Listo.

Sorry, My Cat Fell off the Cupboard

"I have no idea, there must be something wrong with him, it's not like him. Are you alright, puss? Shall I take you to the vet?"

"Give it a couple of days, see how he is then."

"It's odd, he's off his food, keeps stumbling, it must be something, I'll take him Tuesday if he's no better."

Dan was screaming inside. I could not face the awful food they gave him, and his balance was not up to this four-legged thing. He simply could not get the hang of a tail, and how to use it. He hurt all over from the falling, and he was beginning to go slowly insane. How, how, could he get them to understand? He was Dan.

It hurt especially, to notice the excitement they had from the youtube hits rising. They had happened to film him as he tried to jump across to the window sill, and of course, being his first day as a cat, he messed it up. They found it hilarious.

He found it painful and frustrating.

Trying to write them a note, he found it impossible to hold a pen, obviously. He had a great idea, he knocked a box of pencils over and tried to form letters with them. They laughed and cleared them up.

He needed to get back to that bloke's house. But he had no idea where it was. He got out of the cat flap, and everything looked different from down here. He was fairly sure it was on the other side of town. He tried jumping on a bus. Unfortunately it was not possible to see the number, and he rode for a while before jumping off. Now he could not recognise anything of where he was. Come on Dan, what the hell can you do now?

His nose twitched. What is that? Oh, mouse. Before he knew what he had done, he had leapt on it and sunk his teeth into its neck, bringing instant death. Ah shit, thought Dan, this is me.

To Kill a Roadrunner

Where did the roadrunner run before roads? Has our petrol fuelled obsession really provided a natural habitat? Is life better, easier, for this flightless bird now, with cars, with the roads on which to run?

It seems unlikely. The climate is changing, species are becoming extinct. Extracting and burning fossil fuels, we know, is the major contributory factor. Wile E. Coyote wised up. He knew what to do. It may seem that the Roadrunner would be delighted by the increased opportunity for running, and maybe he was. The law of induced demand, however, led to ever more vehicles, cars, trucks, buses, bellowing out vicious earth-choking waste, all day every day.

So Wile E. Coyote final 'got his man'. The Roadrunner is no more

Wile E. Coyote joined the roads lobby.

Loose Laces and Tight Triumphs

Untying the laces they loosened all the way along her back. A sigh escaped in the midst of her deep breaths. Gradually working down, they made exciting progress before the last is breached and her warm body is finally released, a glistening sheen of moisture revealing her thrilled anticipation.

She turns and faces him as she pulls his shirt off his rippling torso, he grins as it catches on his face. That grin. His strong arms tense, his beautiful forearm muscles crease like a marble statue as he lifts her onto him.

They groan, in unison, a perfect triumph of biological engineering operating as one.

Unreplenished Urges

"Pain? We're all in pain."

A lifetime of urges, one of top of another, a layer cake of desires dripping with rich maple syrup, soaking and seeping in, a sweet, sticky, liquid that both refreshes and replenishes. This tower of intense, unstoppable, essential and unavoidable needs never diminishes. However much you eat, gorging away, this cake; you still have it.

And then one day, it stops.

The urge doesn't come back, it hasn't come back. It is a physical manifestation of a cracked, haunted head. It is the oddest of sensations. What was always is no more, what was a driving force, pushes no longer. It is diminished. Redundant. Exhausted. Maybe if one soul is having too much cake, and eating, the next must have none. A balance.

*   *   *   *

So where to next? Find the best, be as good as it can be, look forward, be calm and take yourself with yourself. Don't look behind, don't get stuck, don't drag down, don't lose yourself, don't forget yourself. Simple advice, with unknowable meaning.

But will the urges be replenished then? Will they come back. What manner of sick joke would that be? Urges, replenished yet unfulfillable. A life yet more hollow. What hope for crumbs now? Not one, just an empty silence, to be broken, just as I am broken.

And the cat laughed.

The Founder of Freedom

The knife slipped from her grasp, as she fought her way out of the metro. A glance at the floor to see it clatter to the ground and bounce around before sinking into an elegantly socked ankle. She pushed harder against the crowd.

A deep breath as she surfaces and she was surprised at how relieved she was to be out. Not looking back she strode purposefully, and gracefully. Before long she has cleared the area.

*　　　*　　　*　　　*

On the bench she sat at one end, the other occupied by a woman in a pristine dress, the contact. Why did they have to keep changing?

"I want out."

"You know you can't get out. We need you. You're too precious." A look. "OK I'll look into it. We'll start the process, at least."

A half, uncertain, smile.

Smuggling, Snuggling, or Struggling?

"It's hard; but it's a struggle".

Words I will never forget, words that perfectly encapsulate the difficulty of maintaining positivity in the face of adversity. I first heard them around 1987 up West in London, passed onto to me by an old man (he seemed old to me, maybe he wasn't) living on the streets. I can see him now halfway down the steps of an Underground, he paused half-turned and called to me, by way of encouragement. "It's hard; but it's a struggle."

Inspiring, I think, is what he was aiming at but of course it has a beautifully bleak desperate misery around it. When that is your genuine attempt at cheery, imagine where your life is.

I suppose I cannot begin to liken my lot to his, yet I find myself often thinking of that phrase. It really is hard and it really is a struggle. And it is getting worse, day by day. As I sink into the miserable future I foresaw, another phrase enters my mind, one uttered much more recently.

A little while ago everyone was assuring me, insisting in fact, that it would get better. With time. This made no sense to me at all, why would it? It was the future that was fucked, so how could heading toward it, into it, make it better? It made no sense, and I thought of Pierce Carroll in Penelope Fitzgerald's wonderful *At Freddie's* when he said "No. That won't be the way of it at all."

And then a dear new friend said to me these very wise, and as it turns out, very perceptive, words;

"Sometimes time just makes it worse."

Whispers of Wonder

As soft winds caress
tired, silky sands,
a heart whispers less
forlorn its failed rise.

At once lost, it cries,
then finds to address
anew, ready it flies
and once more, careless.

SUNDAY

This final, additional, section consists of a combined review of a remarkable book, and a striking double portrait.

It includes extracts, quotes and references, without authorisation.

The Summer Book

'You can see for yourself that life is hard enough without being punished for it afterwards' - Tove Jansson

"This breeze is a little cold, are you too cold?" the young woman asked with concern.

She never used to fuss like this, Grandmother thought. Back when she was small enough to be fussed over herself. She never worried about my feelings, or concerned herself with my comfort. In fact, I never fussed over her either. The elderly woman considered for a moment. She preferred those days.

The breeze was light, and the sun was shining. Not at all cold, in fact, for the Gulf of Finland.

After a pause the Grandmother asked "Where did you say you live now? Spain?"

"Yes" Sophia replied, "In Valencia." She added, without knowing why, "That is to say, just outside the city." Grandmother's eyes darted across sharply. "Is that so?" she replied.

The grass gently danced in the breeze. Grandmother thought about the heat of the south that could make her Granddaughter feel this air to be cool.

"You only went to Italy didn't you? Not to Spain." How the young feel they are always the first to experience anything; that cliché ran through the old woman's mind. And I suspect the old always believe they are the first to accuse the young of this, too. She chuckled to herself over the hypocrisy of both youth and age.

The wind was picking up in fact, there were little points of white out on the sea. The two women watched a distant dinghy sail by in a comfortable silence.

Great age comes with responsibilities, one of which is to appear confused. A straightforward manner of achieving this is to converse at tangents. This was something that came very easily to her. "There's a painting in the 'Museo de Belles Artes' in Valencia." She began, relishing the chance to startle her Granddaughter.

Sophia was long used to her ways, and equally delighted in thwarting her, still. "It's 'Museu' now," she explained, "They speak Valencian now. It is called the 'Museu de Belles Arts'. Naturally they all can speak Spanish still, but they prefer their own language."

"What do they do to people who speak Spanish, then?" Grandmother asked, mischievously. Sophia laughed a gentle, indulgent laugh. She was old enough, just, to remember how it was to be a Swedish speaking Finn.

"What about this painting?" She wasn't going to humour the old trickster by being surprised by her knowledge of Valencia.

Grandmother thought back over the years. Memory shortens and flattens but can also lengthen and confuse, of course. Was the emotional memory stronger, or the visual? She decided to try and find out. You ought, at least, to be able to talk about these things.

She took herself back to that place. "It was a long time ago; your mother was still alive. I think she'd have been about ten." I wonder, she thought, I wonder if the pain is still there, "Your grandfather had recently ... I had .... That is to say, well, he had… er," Yes, a little, It is still hard to frame it after all these years, decades, "He had done something he oughtn't have done. The sort of thing people old enough to know better do sometimes, if they want to play at being fools, or being teenagers. Or both. No, maybe not teenagers; they wouldn't be that foolish or cause that much pain." She thought of how teenagers are all lumped together as an absurd, uncaring, pointless group of uncontrollable individuals dangerous to themselves and others. Rather like the very old. It was extremely unfair, she thought – on the teenagers, at least.

Sophia felt herself wince and tense involuntarily. Oh, she thought, she's in pain still. Oh my goodness. It will never fade.

Grandmother continued this disjointed revelation. "We found ourselves in Valencia and for some reason he wanted to visit the gallery. He wandered around chuckling at the ancient religious art; I sat and stared at only one painting." She felt herself there now; surprising herself she found that the smell of the distant gallery overpowered that of the nearby sea. "The background is drab. A dark grey wall, almost deliberately unpleasant. A wall you'd have to work at to keep that unkempt. It was wholly unadorned, the settee was also drab; a nondescript red." The background always struck Grandmother first. "Despite its miserable blankness, the background seemed to speak of family, a warm family."

The younger woman half listened, her mind on something else. She didn't wonder why her ancient relative was telling her this story, or where it might go; she never had. She thought how their pain appeared to resonate; even across this vast time.

"There is a couple on the sofa, he looks rather stern, but

when you go to the gallery make sure you take a good close look at his face. He is sat rather apart from the woman, but his left knee stretches out to touch her, it's an awkward yet loving pose. Not a protective love, but a love of need. There has to be contact. It is a love of equality. The woman has a sweet, smiling face, maybe rather frivolous. But that touch shows the respect he has for her. It is awkward, stiff, but beautiful."

Sophia couldn't remember her grandmother ever talking for so long. Now the older woman lay herself on the sand and granite and appeared to be snoozing.

The Granddaughter thought of this old woman, much younger, sat in anguish staring at this rather plain sounding picture. What did it tell her, she wondered, idly.

But Grandmother was not really asleep, an old trick of course. "It's a Sorolla. A famous Valencian artist, you probably know his bright ones, of people and the sea. Well, he painted lots and lots of portraits. They are framed as is a photograph framed, yet painted in a classical style." That doesn't sound like me she thought, as did Sophia. I must have read it somewhere.

"But you lived a happy life for many years after?" Grandmother felt rather than heard the slight desperation in Sophia's question. She pretended to nap again, so as to allow her grandchild the relief of not having her tear-filled eyes observed.

However old you get, the pain doesn't ease, it seems. "It gets better with time", she soothed; but they both knew she was lying, as the old often do.

The sun had shifted and was burning warmer than ever.

The tide had turned, and the breeze died down. It was calm.

Grandmother sat up unsteadily, and slowly. "After a while you notice that the time the couple spent with the artist, sitting for him, must have been rather jolly fun. What have you been doing yourself, dear? To help?"

Absorbed in her thoughts the precision of the question passed her by, "Oh reading a bit. A lot, actually." She thought of that remarkable little blue book that had helped so much. "I've done something I've never done before, Grandmother, I wonder if that's a good thing? I read the book again."

"It depends. Sometimes new things are only things you've done before but decide to think you haven't." Or maybe that is just when you have lived for so very long, she mused. Too long. "But surely you've often re-read a book!"

"Are you cold?" she asked again, involuntarily, even though she could feel herself that it was rather warm now. "Yes of course. But this was different. I finished and just went back to the beginning and started again. There's no story; nothing happens and everything happens. It is about nothing and about all of life. I read it four times in a row, non-stop. Now I'm reading it to the children. At night. While they sleep."

Grandmother looked sharply up again at her, thinking that sounded rather obsessive. Can you depend on people who just let things happen?

"We had a full life together afterwards, yes. Many years. Maybe I never saw things until they were too late; or he didn't. We didn't have the strength to start again. Or maybe I just forgot the idea along the way, and I didn't even realise

I'd forgotten about it. I think it's wise to keep at it, forgetting isn't always so hard." It becomes second nature, she realised.

Lost for a while inside themselves; the younger woman wondering how to forget, her eyes once more brimming; the older one considering whether it still had the power it once had. She never had understood why speaking the title made her cry, it didn't mean that much to her and it wasn't that moving a phrase, not really. But it always did, every time. She hadn't spoken its name for so many years. "Well, let's see." she thought.

Slowly she stood, leaned on her stick and faced the sea; as dead calm as she could ever remember. "You discover that the couple are his parents-in-law, the mother and father of his wife. They – Sorolla and his wife – had a long and happy marriage, and you can feel the mutual feelings here in this painting. Love and respect given and received from someone else's son. But the title, it is how he chose to name it that tells us. It is not his relationship with them, or even their daughter that he focuses on. His respect and love for them must have been very great indeed for him to highlight their precious position to that which mattered most, what was dearest above all else."

The old woman paused, and the very air sensed it. She knew, across the years (so many years), this still affected as deeply as the first time. Still; she wanted to tell her granddaughter, had to tell her it was going to be alright. She had to speak it now, as the sun shone and everything was fine. Yes, it was fine, yet it was all overshadowed by a great sadness. It was only time on top of time, vanity and a chasing after the wind.

"The painting is called '*Los Abuelos De Mis Hijos*'."

And as the wind picked up again it licked insistently at the tears streaming down the faces of the solitary women, one sitting, one standing, grieving for the past, for the present and for the future.

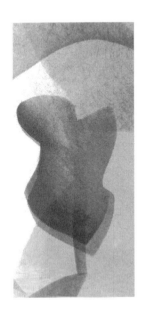 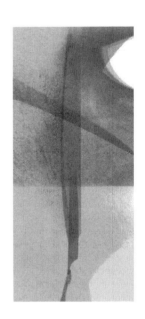

152

INDEX

ABOUT PROMPTED WRITING

This is the second time David's prompted writing has appeared in book form. He works with given random words or phrases from which he had to conjure up a short piece in just ten minutes.

If you wish to challenge yourself to writing in this way, then these 'prompts' are provided and curated by 'M', and can be found every day on the 'Putting My Feet In The Dirt' blog.

His, and others, ten-minute prompted writing continues to appear daily on the 'Prompted For Ten' blog.

Join us - just grab a pen, and ten.

promptedforten.wordpress.com/author/deaddeerblog/
puttingmyfeetinthedirt.com

David also writes on a wide range of topics and these articles and stories can be found on the 'Dead Deer' blog.

deaddeerblog.wordpress.com/